the final case of

JACK GEMINI

T. A. Jenkins

Other books by T. A. Jenkins:

He had a thing for Virgins and other
Stories

ISBN: 9798621036782

the final case of

JACK GEMINI

T. A. Jenkins

the final case of Jack Gemini

1. Woman

I was staring into deep space the night she crashed back into my life.

I was stood at my window, whiskey in hand, and watching the stars. My reflection, a faded, translucent replica of my scruffy unkempt face stared back at me, a slightly better-looking parallel Jack Gemini. The white pinpoints of distant suns freckled his face and head and I charted a course through his thoughts; they weren't saying very much. I sighed. It was going to be one of those nights. I could feel it.

The station was quiet, too quiet, especially considering the storm that would drop into my office that night.

I was up late, head pounding, either from the alcohol or the time, and my case files lay strewn across my desk behind me. I could almost see the papers in the reflection, plastered across the void, a constellation of crimes and misdemeanours to match the stars in my head.

I told myself, way back when, that I'd never leave Earth, never end up on one of these death traps floating in space. But here I was. Earth had changed too much for me since the accident, my accident. That had well and truly fucked things up. Not that things had been going well before, but I'd thought things would improve. It was all bullshit. Chasing philanderers and missing cats was all I was good for now. That, and hearing from weirdos wanting me to look into their alien sightings.

I took another swig of my drink and turned away from the window.

Aliens.

As if.

I slammed the glass on my desk.

That was it for tonight; I was done.

I needed to get some sleep. Or I could head to Sam's bar.

I grabbed my coat and hat from the rack, but my exit was disrupted. Someone was hammering at my office door. I turned to face the interruption. There was a curvy silhouette visible through the glass, curves I would recognise anywhere even though it'd been years since I last laid eyes on them.

Her.

I returned my coat to the hook and moved back to the window.

"Come in," I shouted. "This better not take long."

The hinges whined as the door opened and her heels squeaked across the wooden floor, a black dress hugging her shape and a white shawl draping her shoulders. The devil approached my desk. It was her alright. Her ruby lips flashed me a smile, friendly, deceptive.

"Hello, Jack," she said.

"It's been a long time. Not long enough, if you ask me." I sat in my chair and swung my feet onto the desk. "It's late." I reclined and crossed my fingers on my stomach. "For humans anyway." I nodded to the chair across from me, the cigarette tucked between my lips, and nodded with my head. "Sit."

"I need your help," she said as she sat in the chair opposite. "You're the only one who can." Her eyes did the cute puppy dog act; I wasn't falling for it.

"Really? There's a first time for everything," I said. I lit a cigarette and puffed the smoke toward her. "You must be really desperate to come to this side of Space Station Delta. You not exactly the type to get dirty."

"Earthside is too pretentious for this kind of thing... and you've always managed to get me out of tricky situations before. Back when we were married."

"Bullshit; I was the one who got you into trouble most of the time."

"You and I remember things very differently," she said with a smirk. She lit her own cigarette, her lipstick staining the filter, and puffed. "At the end of the day, you always had my back; you were always there for me."

"We're not married anymore," I told her, "and you wanted nothing to do with me after the accident."

"You were gone for five years, Jack." She crossed her legs and sat back. She shrugged, flicking ash on the floor. "What the hell was I supposed to do? Everyone thought you were dead. I thought you were dead; I moved on."

"I came back."

"I moved on."

"I still came back, Jill. You didn't wait for me."

"Five years was too long to wait; I still had my own life to live. What was I supposed to do?"

"You should've had faith," I said. "You should have had faith that I would come back. And I did. I came back." I glanced over to the bathroom to my right. "Did you know I still have it? My wedding ring?"

"No."

"I keep it safe." I faced the woman. "Locked away." It was in the cabinet above the sink.

"Goddammit, Jack."

"You were the only thing I thought about, during the accident, the whole time."

"You weren't thinking," she replied. "You were trapped; they told me it was like a coma."

"So?"

"You didn't even know any time had passed," she raised her eyebrows at me, "and as far as you were concerned you were in and out. The rest of us..." she sighed, "we had to go the long way around." The woman stubbed out her cigarette on the veneer of my desk. "Pour me a drink, Jack."

I leaned forward and followed suit; my cigarette joined the many chars and stains on the edge of the wood. I stared at her eyes as I picked up the bottle. She watched me. I wanted to know if she loved me, if she still loved me after all these years. I certainly did. Love her, that is. Even after she left me. I felt a little guilty thinking about the woman opposite; I wasn't exactly single. There was Sam. He helped maintain my drinking habit with that little bar of his. I filled my empty glass and pushed it across the table. It was probably for the best that I didn't mention my other lover to Jill.

She lifted the drink and stared at the contents. "You always buy the good stuff." She swirled it around and looked at me. "So," she said, "you'll help me?"

I retrieved a second glass, a clean one, from my drawer and filled it to the brim. I was going to need a big one. I shrugged at her expectant expression. "I'll listen."

"That's not an answer." Her cheeks reddened. Anger. It'd been a long time since I'd seen that face. "Tell me you'll help."

"I told you," I said. I tried to sound mellow and measured, hoping to calm the storm. "I'll listen. Then I'll decide whether to help. Or not." But I couldn't help myself. "It's not like I owe you anything."

"Excuse me?! Who gave you the money to get you back on your feet?"

"And, I'm grateful for that," I said. "I bet my own life insurance policy was a nice windfall for you. It was the least you could do."

"Get bent, Jack."

"You better start talking; I was heading to bed when you arrived."

"You're not fooling anyone. Bed?" she said. "Or is it a bar? Or a cheap tart?"

"Why can't it be all three?"

"You're despicable."

"That's why you married me, Jill." I chugged some whiskey and it burned my throat with its sour tang. "You like a bad boy."

"Bullshit," she snorted a laugh. It was cute. "All you did was peddle stolen goods and involve yourself in illegal betting rings. A dirty cop. It was never anything big. You were charming, but harmless."

"Oh, I'm still charming," I said with a smirk. "And that stuff may be true, but I've changed. You stomped all over my heart and broke me. Everything was different after I came back, back from the accident. You changed."

"Get over yourself, Jack."

I sighed and returned to my reclined position in the chair. I'd forgotten how arguments felt with her. I swung my boots onto the desk and sipped at my whiskey. "You asked for my help."

"You are a pet dick, are you not?" she said. "Isn't that what you do? Help people?"

"For a price, yes. And I haven't decided if I'll take your case yet."

"Understand, and I mean it, this case has nothing to do with me and you or what we had before."

"Stop wasting my time. Out with it."

Jill took a deep breath and huffed. She stared at the ceiling. "It's Howard."

"Your new husband?"

"Jack, Howard and I've been married six years," she said, a particularly stinging barb to my self-esteem. "That's longer than we were together."

I gulped down some whiskey. "Only because you had me declared legally dead."

Jill glared at me.

"Fine," I said, "I'll drop it." I emptied my glass and placed it on the table. "Carry on."

"Howard's missing."

"How long before you declare him dead?" I couldn't help myself. "Scientist, wasn't he?" The look on her face told me to stop but I continued anyway. "Did you lose him to a time vortex too?"

"Jack." She took a deep breath and sighed. "Look, you either take my case or don't. I told you this isn't about us."

"Everything is. To me."

"You sentimental fool."

I shrugged.

Jill pursed her lips and leaned forward. "Then help me. For everything we had." Her painted nails encircled her glass.

I waved my hand, gesturing for her to continue.

"Where do I start?" she said.

"The beginning is usually the best place." I retrieved my notepad from my pocket and took out a pen. It was old fashioned but there was something about the scrape of a nib across paper, albeit fake paper, that helped me think. "How long has he been missing?"

"Two days."

"Have you been to the police?"

"This morning; they filed a report," said Jill. "Told me he's probably off fucking some floozy."

"And is he?"

"No. No, he wasn't... isn't like that."

"Why did you wait so long to go to the cops?" I asked. "You waited until this morning to report him missing."

The woman huffed. "Yes, I did wait," she said. "I was beginning to get worried."

"You still waited two days."

"There... there was good reason... and don't even think this means anything between you and me... but we've been... Howard and I... we've been arguing a lot lately. Sometimes we go days without speaking to each other."

"Trouble in paradise?" She glared at me. "So, you argued before he went missing?"

Jill nodded as she lit up another cigarette. She blew smoke out from the edge of her ruby lips.

"What did you argue about?"

"It doesn't matter; the point is he's missing, and I want you to find him."

I stood and walked to the front of my desk, keeping my eyes firmly focused on her. "If you really want me to find him, then I need to know everything.

All the dirty little secrets, all the faults and flaws, the minutiae." I leaned back on the desk, resting my buttocks against the wood. "Anything could be a clue to finding him."

"You'd love that, wouldn't you? Picking apart my relationship with Howard."

"Do you want me to find him or not?"

She sighed, and a plume of smoke collided with her bosom. "Howard works a lot. Too much. I barely see him during the day." She stared at me. "There were times where I only saw him when he woke me getting into bed at God's knows what time in the morning." Jill pulled a tissue from her cleavage and dabbed her eyes; she carefully avoided smudging her eyeliner. "It's not like I didn't try; I tried every day. He's hardworking and focussed. Committed. It's one of the reasons I married him."

And his paycheque, I thought to myself.

"I'd take him lunch, but he was always too busy to stop. I'd try and meet him after work, but he was always finishing up with something important. I'd make him breakfast, but he'd always rush out the door with barely a bite."

"It sounds like your marriage was on the rocks."

"A rough patch." She stopped dabbing at her tears and looked at me. "People argue, Jack. It doesn't mean their marriage is breaking down, whether you," she jabbed her finger at me, "want it to or not."

"It doesn't matter if I do or don't," I told her. "I'm just trying to get a full understanding of your situation. You never know what will crack the case." I picked up the bottle of whiskey and topped up her glass. "I'm guessing you had an argument about him working too much and you never getting to spend any time with him? Yes?"

"Yes." She sipped at the newly filled drink.

I scribbled in my notebook and paused; I wasn't writing anything important, just making it look like I was. The pause was for effect. I looked into her eyes. "Maybe the police were right about him running away with another woman. Or was it a man?"

"He wasn't like that," she said, "I already told you; he's faithful."

I retrieved my own glass from behind me and topped up the empty glass. I took a hefty swig. "You don't work?"

She shook her head.

"It must have been hard being alone all the time in that big empty house."

"I know what you're suggesting, and I really don't appreciate the accusation."

I took a sip of the amber liquid in my hand. "You didn't cheat on your husband?"

"No, no, I didn't."

"Not even once?"

"No."

"You can't blame me for being suspicious."

"Oh?"

"You cheated on me."

"That was different," she smirked. "Howard and I... it's the real deal."

I didn't believe it, but her words still stung; the words stung deep in my guts. I stood and walked away from her, not wanting her to see my face. She still loved me. I knew it. I'd never stopped loving her even when I was with Sam. And yes, I'd cheated on her in the past, but it was in my nature. She'd done the same. It was in her nature too. We were a perfect match. And she was going to use that to her advantage, use my feelings for her own benefit. I reached the window and stared into the void beyond. I was going to help her.

"Jill," I said, still facing the stars, "what exactly was your husband working on? It must have been pretty important to take him away from someone as smart and as beautiful as you."

"Work. The same thing that never stopped you."

"What was Howard working on?"

"I don't know; it was something to do with a new power source," she said. "Sustainable and pollution-free."

"Sounds too good to be true."

"He was close," she said, "very close to a major breakthrough." I heard the crackle of her cigarette as she took another long drag. "And then, he went missing."

I turned and faced my ex-wife. "You think his work had something to do with his disappearance."

She nodded.

"And you told the cops about your suspicions?"

She nodded again. "They weren't interested."

I sighed. "And tell me, did your husband have any enemies?"

"What sort of question is that?"

"A legitimate one," I said. "You told me he doesn't sleep around so someone else must be behind it. Jealous co-workers? Rivals? Anyone sticking their nose where it doesn't belong?"

"I... I... don't know."

I approached her, skirting my desk and I stood over her as she sat. "Think. I need you to think; it's important. Was there anything unusual happening at your husband's work? Anyone acting strange? It might only be something small, but it could be the key to finding out what happened to Howard."

Jill took a long hard drag of her cigarette, burned to the stub. She threw the used-up filter in the meagre remains of the whiskey and blew the smoke up at me. She looked at me. "Jack," she said, "you need to understand something." She reached around me and placed the glass on the desk. "Howard works in a very competitive industry; there are always rivals. Everyone is trying to solve the energy crisis."

"Any names come to mind?"

"Some. Howard works for Solaris University in Sector Three. Paid tenure."

I bet.

"He had free rein; the University trusted him. Especially considering the big companies that always liked to sponsor his research. There was a pretty big one bankrolling his current project; I just don't remember who."

"Give me some examples."

"Electrodyne," she counted with her fingers, "Calesthetica, Elongate, Tribeca Systems... they're the main ones it could be."

"Do you mean Tribeca Corp?"

"No, Tribeca Systems."

"I'm sure they were called Tribeca Corp," I said. "Even before I got stuck in that time vortex."

"No, they've always been Tribeca Systems."

"My mistake." Another name stuck out. "And Elongate?"

"You might remember them as Elongax back in the day."

"I remember," I told her, "they used to supply the police force with their uniforms and vehicles; they've never been particularly interested in new tech. I'm pretty certain nothing has changed."

"Do you think one of those companies is behind my husband's disappearance?"

"No, but it's a start." I jotted down the four company names in my notepad; I circled Tribeca. I was sure they were the ones in charge of power generation on Space Station Delta. "It might be nothing."

Jill grinned at me. "You're going to take my case."

"It'll cost you."

"You're going to exploit a woman in a vulnerable state, worried for her missing husband? Well, Jack, you've really hit a new low."

I shrugged. "I've got bills to pay. And you want me to prioritise your case over my others, yes?"

Jill rolled her eyes, the same way she always used to whenever she didn't get her own way. Her breasts rose and fells as she emitted a deep sigh. "I want you to find Howard." She clutched her purse and it clicked open beneath her fingers. "I'm transferring you your initial fee now." She retrieved her SmartBoy and tapped along the screen. "You'll be rewarded handsomely when you find him. More, if he's still alive." She returned the device back in her purse. "Done." The woman stood, her body close to mine. I could smell the sweet fruity aroma of her favourite perfume, the one I always bought her for her birthday. Had she worn it on purpose? To manipulate me? Or did she still love me? A small part of me prayed for the latter. Her bosom pressed against me for a moment and I yearned for her. I wanted her. I missed her. Her ruby lips pursed. "I trust you will do your best," she breathed.

I nodded and swallowed hard.

"Good." She stepped away from me and smiled. "I'll be in touch."

"When?" I replied a little too quick, too eager; I hadn't meant to sound desperate.

"Soon," she said. "Keep this under wraps; it could be dangerous."

I nodded.

The woman sauntered to the door, her hips and bum swayed as her stilettos clicked a path to the exit. She paused. "It was good to see you again, Jack. In spite of the circumstances"

She left, and I was alone in my office once more.

I needed a goddamned drink.

the final case of Jack Gemini

2. Bar

      I headed out and into the streets of Sector Six. I pulled my coat closer around me. That was the problem with living Star Side they always skimped on the atmospheric controls. Sectors One to Four always got the best treatment, being Earthside; that was where all the rich people lived, and they paid for good living. Not like the other Sectors. We were the scum of Space Station Delta. Well, second only to the scum of Sector Seven. Low priority. The best choice for power conservation; we were in an energy crisis after all and it wasn't as if we needed as much power as Earthside, not with all their energy sucking luxuries. I sighed to myself. I wished we had the luxuries of Earthside. It was too chilly here.

      The streets were quiet and so were the bars that lined the pavement, even for this time of night. Maybe it was a weekday; being a self-employed alcoholic I'd always lose track of my days. I checked my watch. Wednesday. You'd think this would be the busiest night.

I made my way down the steps leading to Hell, my favourite haunt and owned by my current lover, Sam. I glanced at the paving bricks beneath my feet with each tread. Every slab bore an inscription, and I personally found them a little on the nose, but I always made a point of reading at least one every time I came here. There were things like 'hired a friend but he had no experience,' and 'gave a homeless man money and he bought drugs.' Who'd ever come up with the idea when the bar was founded must've found it pretty funny at the time, but it really wasn't. 'Giving my dog treats to make her happy; she got fat and died.' Yes, that one was certainly a barrel of laughs.

I could hear music, a dreary and longing tune, coming from inside as I reached the door.

Maybe I should add 'helping Jill' to the list behind me.

I entered the bar. Bathed in a vulgar crimson light, familiar and gaudy Halloween decorations greeted me; it was like this all year round. Themed. I hated it.

"You're not playing it again, Sam?" I said to the bartender of the almost empty room. There were three or four regulars, me being one of them, propping up the bar.

"I love this song," said Sam. "It reminds me of you." He winked at me.

"What?" I took up my usual stool. "Sad and depressing?"

"It's romantic, Jack." He leaned over the bar and planted a kiss on my cheek. "I don't care if you like

18

it or not; I do." He placed glass in front of me and filled it with whiskey. "It's about a man who cares more about his work than his lover."

"Who sings it? The lover?" I took a sip of the smooth liquid; it was better than the store-bought stuff in my office. "Or the man?"

"The man," said Sam. He placed his elbows on the bar and looked at me. His long black hair was still in its neat waves despite me knowing he'd been working all day. "He longs for something he's missed out on."

"Yep," I said, "sounds sad and depressing."

"Could be worse."

"How?"

"He might not have a lover, someone who loves him."

I sighed. "Are you trying to tell me something, Sam?"

He stood upright and grinned. "You work too hard, Jack."

"Don't I know it." I retrieved my cigarettes from my coat and pulled out a white stick. Sam offered me a light and I took it gladly.

"You also smoke and drink too much."

I raised an eyebrow in replay and took another swig of the whiskey.

"Actually," said Sam, "you're drinking is keeping me in business."

"It's just an excuse to see you." I smiled at the man. "Why else would I come here?"

"You should come over more often and stop working so late."

"Talking of work, you'll never guess who just showed up in my office tonight."

"Mrs Lafferty lost her cat again?"

"No," I said. "Jill."

Sam sighed. "Really, Jack? You know I don't like it when you talk about her."

"Jealous?" I flashed him a grin; he didn't buy it.

"I just think it's time you moved on; you've been pining for her for years. What did she want, anyway?"

"She offered me a new case."

"And you took it?"

I nodded. "Why wouldn't I? It's good money."

"Bullshit," he said. He waggled his finger at me. "You're letting your old life get in the way of your new one. You should've told her to bugger off."

"Jill and me, we've got a lot of history."

"That's exactly how it should stay. History."

He walked away and I watched his thin frame from behind as he served one of the other patrons. He was another one I was letting get away. Like Jill.

Maybe Sam was right; I was allowing my ex-wife to prevent me moving on. Except that wasn't quite true. Not after she showed up tonight. It brought back memories. Old feelings. I imbibed some more alcohol and took a long hard drag of my cigarette. Something from my past, something that used to be central to my life had collided headfirst with my work in the present.

And her new husband was missing.

New husband.

Married for six years.

I'd only been seeing Sam for one, maybe two years. On and off.

I emptied the glass and lifted it for a refill. Sam was still chatting with someone else in the bar and I was happy to wait; he might still be pissed at me for bringing up Jill. I'd soon bring him round. I sucked on the cigarette in my mouth and looked around the bar. There were familiar faces in here tonight. Sam was serving the old woman who came inside to keep warm and drink herself to oblivion. Just down the bar from me, another woman. A high-flying executive type. A wannabe, at least. There was no way she was on good money to live down here in Sector Six. I sighed. I suppose there was that completely impractical saying about dressing for the job you want. It wasn't going to work, I thought to myself as I admired her upmarket suit, there was no way someone Earthside would hire you when they find out you were from Sector Six. Nice clothes though; they looked expensive.

Sam topped up my glass with a sly smile; he couldn't stay mad at me for long. Me and him, it was all just fun. I returned the smile. Fun. I'd have to take him out somewhere nice.

I looked down at the filled container in my hand. More whiskey. Just what I needed.

The bartender moved to the third patron, a man from my life before the accident. This night was becoming haunted; my past was coming back to slap me in the face.

I stubbed out my cigarette in an ashtray on the bar and stood. I walked over to my old friend and partner, a face from when I was a cop.

"Hello Robert, it's been a while." I took up a stool next to him.

"Yes," he said, "yes, it's been too long."

"I don't think I've seen you since before the accident."

"No." He sipped his own drink. It looked like vodka; it wasn't the type of drink I would choose. The last time I'd drunk vodka I'd blacked out and ended up naked in a back alley in Sector Seven. That was a good night.

I eyed Sam who took the hint to leave us be. Work related. Sam understood and was used to it. I really needed to take him out sometime, make up for things. "I was going to come down the station tomorrow."

"It's probably best you don't," said Robert. "That's partly the reason I'm here."

"I didn't think you were here for a catch-up," I said. "How's the wife by the way?"

"Still dead."

"Shit, sorry, I forgot."

"It's been nearly a decade, Jack. I don't expect you remember everything."

I took a large gulp of my whiskey. "Still with the police?"

Robert nodded. "Head of Sector Three division."

"Good for you!" I patted his back. "I remember you wanting that back on Earth. When we worked together."

"I would never have gotten this far if we were still partners, Jack."

"Never a truer word spoken," I said as I raised my glass and Robert clinked his against mine. "I was a goddamned awful cop."

"Nah, you were good enough," he said. "Just a little jaded and misguided."

"I think 'dirty' is the word you're looking for." I pulled out my cigarettes and offered my former partner one.

"I quit."

"Really?" I lit up my own. "You used to smoke more than me."

"I had to," said Robert. "Promotions are much easier to reach when you're not hacking up phlegm when climbing the ladder."

"Fair enough." I took a long drag and blew the smoke away from him and toward the bar where it collided with a horned devil mask. Fitting. "So, what brings you to my neck of the woods?"

He looked me dead square in the eyes. "You know why."

I drew in a deep breath. "She swung by my office this evening."

"I gathered she would." He took another swig of his vodka. "She always runs to you when she's out of options. You're going to help her, aren't you?"

I nodded. "It's a paid gig."

"You'd do it for free. For her."

"I need the money."

"Bullshit," said Robert. He turned to face me. "I know things between us weren't great even before the accident. After we fell out, after the argument, I swore I would never help you again, but I want to help you now. Make amends. And I'm telling you, officially and unofficially, you're better off out of this mess."

"Are you after her yourself?" I said somewhat in jest. "She's a paid client; I'm not going to turn down the kind of money she was offering for me to find her husband, and it's not as if your lot were any help to her. She told me the cops told her he was off fucking someone else." I paused. "Wait, what argument? The last time I saw you, you were just about to be transferred to Sector Three."

"I saw you just after my transfer was made official," said Robert. "You accused me of deserting you. You were drunk at the time."

"I must've been very drunk; I don't remember that at all."

"You were absolutely hammered," he said. "You came banging on my apartment door demanding to speak to me, barged in and started berating me. You said some pretty awful things. Some of them were true."

"I don't remember. Maybe the time vortex messed with my brain. But if it happened, then I'm very sorry."

"It was a long time ago," said Robert. "It's forgotten." He took my cigarette from my hand and took a long drag. He let out a big sigh with the smoke.

"I told you I was making amends." He handed the cigarette back. "I'm here to help."

"You could help by answering a few questions."

"Jack, it would be a good idea not to ask those questions."

I emptied my glass and waved to Sam for a refill. "I can't let this go, Robert. Not when Jill's involved."

Our drinks were topped up before my former partner began talking again; it was obvious he was nervous about anyone overhearing. His tone changed and his voice lowered.

"You know what Howard was working on, right?" he whispered.

I nodded. "A new power source."

"More or less," said Robert. "The company bank rolling his research is leaning in on this hard; you don't want to get noticed by them."

"Do you mean Tribeca Systems? Are they ones funding him?"

Robert sighed. "I can't tell you that."

"And why aren't the police getting involved? Was that your decision?"

"No. Message from above," said Robert. He pointed up. "I told you; they are leaning hard. We were told to keep everyone away from the case. Including Jill. They don't want this getting out; the power crisis is too important."

"So now you've got the fancy job, you don't want to jeopardise it?"

"I'm jeopardising my job just talking to you."

"And Jill? Why is she being kept out of this?"

"It's for the best. She might blab."

"Instead of trying to find her missing husband your lot drove her to me with tales of extramarital activities."

"That's why I'm here tonight," he said. "I honestly didn't think she would go to you. Unintended consequences." He took a drink of vodka. "It's a good thing I had her tailed, isn't it? And before you say anything, it was for her protection. Professor Lowe's disappearance is big news."

"Did you tell anyone you came to me?"

"No, and I'm keeping it under wraps that Jill came here. The official report will say she stayed at home after speaking with the police. I want as little complications around this as possible."

"Because of your career?" I stubbed out my cigarette and offered Robert a fresh one. He took it without hesitation or rejection. I lit it for him and followed suit with my own. "If your career's so important, why are you getting involved?"

"History." He puffed the cigarette.

"We've got a lot of that."

The other man nodded. "Too much." He blew out a plume of smoke. "I'm saying this again; you don't want to be involved in whatever's going on here."

"It's too late, Robert; I was involved as soon as she was."

"You're too much of a sucker for that dame."

I sighed and took a large swig of my whiskey. "Don't I know it."

My former partner downed his drink. "I need to get going; it's late."

I nodded to him as he stood.

"Take care of yourself, Jack."

I nodded again.

"I mean it," he said.

I turned to him, and I don't know what instincts made me do it, but something felt wrong; I jumped to my feet and tackled him to the floor.

And then everything to my left exploded.

The windows of the bar burst inwards, glass and wood shattered and shook; debris and dust became missiles, firing into the room. I felt shrapnel splatter across my back. Something pierced my coat and my skin. Pain. I fell on top of Robert. We hit the floor together and he grunted as I knocked the air from his lungs. Smoke filled my nose, burning, acrid. My ears rang and Sam's sappy love song played, distant and mumbled.

I didn't want to lose him either.

I clambered to my feet, disconnecting myself from Robert's body. He said something but I couldn't hear him. Dizzy. Eyes and breath on fire. I staggered and fell against the bar and my fingers shifted rubble and dust. My side hurt. I tried to focus but I only saw blurred lights; smoke and dust danced through the air. My torso was wet. Something trickled along my skin. The pain made it harder to move; deep and cutting, it spread through me. I stumbled and tried to steady myself to avail.

I went down.

I fell.

I felt myself knock into a stool and recoil to the floor.

The music grew clearer as I lay there, the wound in my side bleeding out and the smoky stench growing strong. I heard the lyrics.

Love is lost but not forgotten...

I opened my eyes.

Sam's beautiful face looked down at me and everything faded away.

3. Hospital

I woke to an unfamiliar ceiling, white and cast with shadows. I felt groggy. Meds. I recognised the almost supernatural feeling flowing through my muscles and bones; this wasn't the first time I'd been in hospital. And it wouldn't be last.

I turned my head, following the grout between the tiles to the curtained window. There was someone else in the room. I could smell perfume. Or aftershave.

A crumpled silhouette was piled into a chair in front of the closed curtains; it was hard to make out who it was through the filtered light from outside, and the blankets hid their sleeping, but familiar, form.

"Jill?" My voice was quiet; I could barely hear the words myself, nevermind the figure keeping my healing body company. "Jill?" They didn't move. "Jill?" I croaked, louder this time.

The shape stirred, groaning, and I realised who it was.

"Sam?" I was glad he hadn't seemed to hear me call out... to her.

"Hmmm?"

"Sam," I repeated.

The blankets slid down and the tired and unshaved man was revealed. "You're... you're awake," he stumbled. He stood, dropping the fabrics that had enveloped him to the floor. He rushed to my side and I felt his arms encircle me. It hurt. He hugged me, hard, and his warmth felt good. I'd missed him and I felt guilty I'd thought about Jill. I really had missed him. But the hug still hurt. "I've been so worried," he whispered. His breath tickled my ear, a pleasant feeling, distracting me from the pain of his hug.

"You can let go now," I said. He withdrew; Sam and I had been on and off for a long time, and I was glad he'd been here for me while I slept. "How long have I been out?"

Sam pulled open the curtains and light flooded the room from the streetlights outside. I winced at the intrusion. "About a day, I think," said Sam. "You took a large chunk of spiroglass to the torso."

"Why the hell did you have goddamned spiroglass for the windows in the bar?"

"You know... just in case."

"In case of what?" I pulled myself up, struggling to move the pillows behind me. "Spiroglass is only good for lasers! No-one has money for that kinda firearm in Sector Six. And that stuff is fragile as fuck for anything else!"

"Oh, alright, it was cheap," said Sam. He helped me sit up, fluffing my pillows and adjusting them behind my back. "Do you need some water?"

I nodded. My throat felt like a hooker's after a lucrative night.

"I hope you're not going to keep bringing trouble to my bar, Jack." He handed me a glass. "My insurance is high enough as it is."

"How is the bar? Much damage?"

"It's mostly whole; the windows are completely gone."

"I'm not the only one that causes trouble in that place," I sipped at the water. "No offence, but it isn't exactly a high-end establishment." I cleared my throat. "Although, there was that fancy looking bird in there tonight."

"I didn't see anyone like that, just the usual crowd." Sam smirked. "Anyway, I can ban troublemakers," he said. "I'm not going to get rid of you, despite how you treat me sometimes."

"You've never made any complaints before."

He laughed. "No, no I haven't." His face turned serious. "But you could've died." He ran his fingers along my cheek. "I've been thinking, and don't freak out. I don't want to lose you; you're important to me, Jack. I want to take this to the next level."

"It was only a bit of spiroglass; hard to get out but not life-threatening."

"You're not listening; I'm serious," said Sam. He was close, he stood over my prostrate form. "This

31

casual stuff is holding us back; I want to go on a proper date with you."

"We've been on proper dates." The miasma of the meds was beginning to fade, and the realism of reality was hitting hard. "Lots of dates." My torso ached inside and out; it felt like someone had been digging about in my entrails. They probably had.

"Dates? You mean getting drunk and fucking?" He crossed his arms. "You only come to see me when you're horny. Or depressed."

"All the time, then?" I grinned.

Sam rolled his eyes and sighed. "You still love her, don't you?"

"Who?" Shit.

"You know who I'm talking about."

"Not this again, Sam. You shouldn't be so jealous. She's married. I don't love her; I love you."

"Then, why did you take her case? You could've said no."

"She needed me."

"I need you, Jack."

"I don't see how Jill has anything to do with our relationship."

"You don't get it, do you? You really don't understand why I'm so cut up about this."

"Sam, I…"

My on and off lover walked over to where he'd been sitting. He retrieved a bag from beside the chair. "This was your last chance, Jack and you don't need me, want me, here anymore," he said. He was still facing away. "You're all recovered now." He kept his gaze away from me as he headed to the door. "Enjoy being with her." He slammed the door behind him.

I lay there listening for his footsteps, but I could only hear the sounds of a busy hospital; nurses and doctors rushing past, voices over the tannoy directing them here and there. Patients flatlined.

So did my heart.

It was only casual though, right? Then why did I feel so goddamned shit about Sam leaving? I should've committed, moved on from Jill. Sam was a good guy. And I used him up. I could only hope he would forgive me.

His bar was the best place in Sector Six to get a decent drink.

Well, maybe not the best. The cheapest. And closest.

Goddamn it. Why couldn't I just be straight with him? Sam was the closest thing I had to a relationship and there was no doubt in my mind that he'd stayed by my side the whole time I was unconscious. He cared for me. Why couldn't I care about him as much as he did for me? I could make it work. We could make it work. I could leave my past behind me and move on, forget about everything that happened between me and Jill, move forward. Sam was a good guy. Me, not so much, but I could be better, do better, for him.

I sighed.

It was a pipe dream. Me and Sam would never work; the world was too shit and so was I. I'd just contaminate him with my filth. Just like I did to Jill. I'd ruin his life and drive him away. I'd already ruined his bar; there was no doubt that the explosion was somehow linked to my newest case. It couldn't have been an accident. Robert had almost explicitly told me there was some sort of cover-up, that someone high up was calling the shots on this whole thing. No accident.

The only thing that worried me was whether the target was me. Or Robert.

I needed to speak to him. Wherever he was. And he wouldn't like it. He'd clearly told me not to get involved. And he'd better be goddamned grateful; I saved his life. I shifted position; the pain in my side reminded me to use that against him. I was in the hospital because of Robert. I could use it as leverage.

There was a knock at the door, an unwelcome intrusion to my thoughts, and a round face appeared.

"I hope we're not disturbing you," said the cop. He barged his way into my room. A woman followed. "We need to ask you some questions." Both wore the familiar navy uniform, almost military, that I'd once worn. "About the explosion."

"Now is not a good time," I said. I really didn't want to talk to these jokers, the big man with the overly nice face and the fresh-faced woman accompanying him were not welcome. I needed to get out of here.

"We won't keep you long, promise." The cop smiled a fake smile. "I'm Detective Suede and this is my partner, Detective Johnson."

I felt my eyes roll in my head; I didn't need this right now.

The door closed behind them and the pair strode to my bedside; they were trying to look friendly, but it was coming across as sinister. Fake grins and bubbly gestures. I wondered for a moment if Robert had sent them, or someone higher.

"How're you feeling, Mr Gemini?" said Suede. He flipped open a notebook. "All healed up?"

"I feel like shit."

The cop's face turned serious. "So, you won't be going on any holidays soon then?"

"What?"

"Not planning on leaving the station, are you Mr Gemini?"

"I don't see what that's got to do with you," I said. "I think you need to explain what's going on; am I under investigation?"

"Perhaps," said Suede.

"Get to the point," I said, "I'm in pain and I'm not in the mood for this bullshit."

The bulbous cop sighed. "Tell me about what happened the night of the explosion."

"I was having a quiet drink in my local and something exploded in the doorway. And if you hadn't noticed, shrapnel from the blast put me in this damned place."

"Who were you there with?"

I paused. Did they know Robert was there? My old friend had come to warn me about my newest case, and he wasn't supposed to be in the bar; there was a conspiracy. Undoubtedly. And if I told them he was there it might cause problems with my investigation. But these idiots, they had to know he was there; why else would they be asking me?

"An old friend," I said.

"Robert Grimes."

I stayed quiet. So, Robert hadn't sent them.

"Mr Gemini," said Johnson, the clearly newbie cop, "it's in your best interests to cooperate with us; this is a murder investigation after all."

"Murder? What's that got to do with me? Go talk to Robert; he's division head in Sector Three. One of you guys."

Suede raised his eyebrows at me. "You don't know?"

"Should I?"

"Robert Grimes is dead."

"Bullshit," I said. The explosion was seared in my memory. "I saved his life." I clutched my side, my injury responding to my claims. "I shielded him from the blast; he wasn't hurt, I was."

"That doesn't change the fact that he's dead," said Detective Suede. "He was found at the scene, burnt and battered by the explosion. We think someone had it in for him. Tell me, Mr Gemini, has there been any violence at Hell before?"

"Nothing that isn't the norm."

"The norm?"

"It's a dive bar." I needed a cigarette. "It's got its usual share of bar fights and troublemakers."

"And, are you one of the troublemakers? We saw the owner, Sam Whittle, leaving this room. He looked pretty upset."

"That has nothing to with it," I said. "Sam and I... we're... we were seeing each other." I felt a little ashamed of the way I'd treated him. "Listen, I still don't believe Robert is dead; he was fine before I fell unconscious."

"Have you ever been involved with, or instigated any violence in the bar?"

"No."

"You have a history of assault."

"Looked me up before you came in here, did you? I'm a private investigator and..."

"You used to be a police officer."

"...and sometimes things can get violent. Do you know what happens when you tell someone their significant other is cheating? I've been arrested before. Self-defence."

"Multiple times."

"Yes," I said. "I don't regret them either; I'd rather not be beaten to a pulp. Or dead." I sighed. "Look, I know you guys don't like people in my profession, I've been there myself, but cut me some slack; Robert is an old friend. We used to be partners. Why would I want to kill him? And if it was the explosion was the cause, why would I be in the bar when it happened?"

Suede cleared his throat. "We're not accusing you of anything. Just keeping our options open."

"I don't particularly like your tone."

Detective Johnson stepped forward and removed her cap; she held it against her chest with both hands. "Mr Gemini," she said, "we're not here to attack you; we just need your help that's all."

"I can only tell you what I saw."

"That's all we ask."

"Sir," said Suede, "would you be willing to come to down to the station and give us a statement?"

"Now?" I swung my arms up and down my body; it hurt, but I think I got the point across. "I'm a little indisposed at the moment."

"When you're healed," said the large detective, "come and see us." He pulled out a card and placed it on the bedside table. "Just don't wait too long." He patted the card with his fingers. "Okay?"

"Thank you, Mr Gemini," said the woman cop with an attempt at a grin, "we don't want to have to come looking for you." She winked. How predictable. They were trying to get me on their side. It was suspicious. The two cops seemed too fresh. Incompetent. I got the feeling they didn't really know what they were doing.

"I'll be sure to stop by," I said with a forced smile. "Now, if you don't mind, I'd like to get a little bed rest." I winced, theatrically. "I'm in a lot of pain." My side genuinely hurt.

"Spiroglass can be particularly nasty stuff," said Suede. "I got sliced by some a couple of years back. That stuff should be banned." He turned to his partner and gestured to the door with his head. "Come along."

"It was nice meeting you," said Johnson.

"Likewise," I lied.

Suede followed Johnson to the door and paused. "Mr Gemini?" He turned to face me. "Do you know why Robert Grimes was at the bar? It's a little out the way for him."

"No, but it was a nice surprise seeing him." The cop studied my face. "A blast from the past," I said, pun not intended. "I hadn't seen him in about eight years." I wasn't going to give anything away. "We had a nice catch up." I raised my eyebrows. "Is that all?"

"Yes, yes, thank you again, Mr Gemini." He gave a knowing look to his partner who'd stood just beyond the door watching the interaction. "Don't forget to come visit the police station."

"I won't," I said.

And with that, I was left alone with my thoughts.

I turned, my face scrunched up as pain shot through my torso, and reached for the business card.

It was clear to me that Suede and Johnson were suspicious of the night's events, but they were ignorant; they didn't know enough of what was going on. They didn't know why Robert was there. They didn't seem to know anything. I was certain they didn't know about my newest case.

But why were they here? Were they sent? Or were they just jobsworths?

I needed a cigarette.

Or a drink.

Or both.

I pushed myself upright, forcing myself through the pain, wincing. Spiroglass was a pain in the ass. A pain in my side. My eyes watered. Goddamn it, I definitely needed to patch things up with Sam or I was never going to move on from Jill; I wasn't sure if wanted to. I threw off the blanket, much to my discomfort, and twisted my bare legs over the side of the bed. My side screamed at the movement; I steadied myself, pressing against the bandages beneath my hospital gown and I shuffled myself into a seated position, feet hanging above the floor.

I stared at the card Detective Suede had handed to me; it was just an official card with the station's address and telephone number. Suede's name was printed at the bottom.

I put the card back on the table.

Like hell was I going to give a goddamned statement to those clods.

There were more important things to worry about, important things to do.

First, a cigarette.

I turned, painfully, and pressed my thumb against the sensor on the bedside table. The drawer slid open. Thankfully Sam had stowed my cigarettes and lighter in there; he knew me too well. My SmartBoy was safely tucked in there too.

I stood. I wobbled. I felt weak and exhausted, dizzy. The medication was still coursing through me despite my tender torso. A draft tickled the opening in the back of my gown and the hairs on my skin stood steadier than my own two feet. I needed to find a coat. I took a step forward and my bare feet slid across the cold floor.

There was a closet just across from me and my honed detection skills told me what I needed resided within. I shuffled forward.

I caught sight of my ghastly reflection in the window; I looked worse than ever.

The closet opened with a press of my thumb and revealed my clothes from that night; the musty smell hit me straight away. It would've been nice if the hospital had dry cleaned them for me. I grabbed my jacket and carefully wrapped it over my injured body. I threw my cigarettes in the pocket. I took a step back. I'd need shoes too. There was no point going all the way outside in bare feet. Not in this sector; I might catch something.

I stepped into my shoes, sockless, and made my way to the hallway outside. A nurse directed me to the smoking area; she gave me a judgmental glance, but I couldn't be bothered to argue with her. I made my way down the hall. Doctors and orderlies passed, patients shambled, like I did, walking corpses trapped in this godforsaken place, and some were wheeled. Hospitals were always a sorry state of affairs. Depressing. People dying. People waiting for death.

A goddamned cigarette would thankfully bring me one step closer.

I looked up and followed the signs to the exit. Another caught my eye.

'Morgue.'

Another destination I needed to be.

The cigarette could wait; there was someone else's death more important than my own.

What those two cops had told me about Robert, it didn't sit right.

I headed along the corridor until I reached an elevator. The morgue was in a basement, but how to get there? I entered the small chamber and looked at the two hundred buttons on the wall; I'd almost forgotten that this was one of the largest hospitals Space Side of the station. I pressed the basement button in hope. Nothing. I noticed a swipe pad next to the buttons. Goddammit. I couldn't risk hacking the wiring to get what I wanted; it would draw too much attention. I needed the passkey and there was only one way to get one. It was time for a little journey.

I pressed the button for floor 200.

This may have been a mistake.

I was stuck in that lift for almost an hour. It was painful and exhausting. The drugs had worn off, and it took every ounce of my strength not to collapse. But I managed it. I waited until I was alone with one of the doctors, one with a key card in an easy to pickpocket position, and I swiped my passage to the lower levels. Now, all I had to do was wait. Again. Until the doctor left.

I took my chance as soon as I could.

I reached the basement and exited into the hallway; it was quiet. Good. That would make my task all the easier. And creepier. There was something really disconcerting about being alone in the silent, not well lit, corridor, surrounded by probably dozens of rooms filled with the dead. The last time I came here, about a year ago, I wasn't on my own. It had been for a missing person case and I needed to know who'd been brought in, my prey, or someone else. Sam had come along. To keep me company. His skittishness had eased my own and his company had been comforting. He had been right; I needed to take our relationship more seriously. I couldn't keep my heart in the past. With her.

I crept forward. I needed to find the reception in order to find Robert; I doubted he was still in Autopsy, given how quickly the hospital usually processed stiffs, but I had to be sure.

The desk was ahead, quiet like the rest of the floor. It was strange. I always thought the morgue would be busier in a place like Sector Six, especially because Sector Seven didn't have its own hospital and that was place was ten times rougher than my home Sector.

The terminal at the desk pointed me to Storage; it seemed the butchers of the morgue had found all they could from his corpse. There was no point trying to break into the reports; I had to see him for myself.

Suede and Johnson, they'd said his body was burnt and battered. It didn't make sense. The explosion hadn't been big enough to cause that much damage; I was relatively unburnt. And I'd saved Robert's life. The spiroglass hit me, not him. And that didn't kill me. How could Robert be dead?

I needed to see the body. That is, if it was still recognisable. Burnt and battered could mean anything and for all I knew, he'd been completely disfigured.

He'd survived worse than this. I thought back to a case we'd worked on together, back before the accident. When we were partners. We'd raided a crime syndicate on the top floor of a building back on Earth and, rather than being caught, they perps had done something stupid.

I reached Storage and opened the door.

The criminals knew they'd been caught, amateurs that they were, and thought they could escape by doing something big.

I made my way to the lockers, where the bodies were kept. Number 2096.

The whole building had come down; they'd set off explosives throughout the structure and tried, unsuccessfully, to escape with a helipod.

I cracked open the locker. The dead, cold soles of the body's feet stared at me. Something wasn't right here.

That building had collapsed with me and Robert still inside.

I slid out the tray holding the body. It was Robert. At least, what wasn't charred and burnt resembled him.

We'd survived the collapse, only a few cuts and bruises for myself, and maybe one or two broken bones.

As soon as I'd opened the locker, seen his feet, I knew something was wrong. No scars. I placed my hands on his left knee. No. Strange. It didn't feel right. Goddammit. I needed to be sure. I rummaged through the drawers of a nearby desk and found, not a scalpel, a penknife. It would have to do. The pallid, stiff flesh wasn't easy to cut but I managed. I cut deep. Down to the bone.

Bone.

That case we'd worked, I'd survived it relatively unscathed. Robert... his leg had been shattered to pieces. Bone had been replaced with metal. Robert had, should have, artificial bones beneath the skin.

There was only bone.

the final case of Jack Gemini

4. Office

It was almost a day later when I returned to my office. I was mostly healed, and there was very little pain, just an ache in my side. The office was my both home and workplace; I was glad to be back.

It was evening by the time I reached the doors to the apartment block and the Sector lights were beginning to dim. Those running the station didn't think the lower classes, the poorer people, needed much light at night-time; it was all for the cause of power conservation, of course, and it didn't matter if the have-nots didn't have, as long as the richer areas didn't complain. I climbed the stairs to my office. Even the common areas were subject to the waning illumination.

I reached my door.

It was fake. Fake wood, at least. Which, in my opinion, was a complete waste of time; wood was still a thing, before and after my accident; it was cheaper to make a plastic imitation than grow more trees. It was goddamned bullshit.

I slid the key in the lock. I paused. It was unlocked. I was sure I'd locked it before I went to Sam's bar. I never forgot to lock my door. Too many important documents. Evidence. And my expensive whiskey collection.

I listened, checking if an intruder still remained, quenching my curiosity and paranoia. There was nothing but the usual hum of the lights and the drunken party that always carried on down the hall. I pushed open the door and I felt the hairs along the back of my neck stand on end. The hinges creaked as the fake wood swung inwards, slowly revealing the darkened office.

I stared into the gloom; I couldn't even see the stars through the far window. I took a step and reached my hand to the left. The hat-stand. I gripped the metal stem and lifted it; it wasn't heavy but would be useful to fend off an intruder. I moved into the dark room.

I took a breath and held the hat stand out in front of me.

I was ready.

I felt along the wall for the switch. Found it. The room was enlightened, and so, was I.

Empty.

The paperwork on my desk was still strewn across its surface, accompanied by two empty glasses from that night, the night she visited my office. The same night I ended up the damned hospital.

I moved further into my office. I looked to the shelves on my left. Nothing unusual. And to my right, the door to the bathroom. Closed, but that wasn't unusual; there was nothing quite like the smell of a freshly used toilet to put off paying customers. I relaxed. I was alone. I dropped the hat stand to the floor and its legs clicked against the fake wooden slats.

I circled the desk, ignoring the stand I'd left waiting at the centre of the room. I'd put it back later. For now, it was time to get knee-deep in research. I needed to make a proper start on Jill's case.

The missing scientist, Professor Howard Lowe.

The explosion in Sam's bar.

The apparent death of Robert.

There had to be a connection, a thread linking all three events.

I sat down and retrieved some whiskey from my drawer. I topped up my dirty glass; there'd was no alcohol in the hospital, only drugs, and drugs didn't give me the same buzz. I took a sip. This goddamned case was going to be the death of me.

I lit a cigarette and glanced at the papers in front of me; I needed to put these aside for now. This newest case, while, at first, a chore, was become more intriguing than all the crap I'd been working on. It was now my priority. For Jill. And her hefty bank balance. I toasted the air. This case was bringing out the detective in me again. I needed to solve it. I needed it. I was beginning to feel that sense of curiosity that tickled the back of your brain. I needed answers. I was going to crack this case like a walnut.

But where to start?

Robert Grimes? That was no way that was him in the morgue, but it was a bloody good lookalike.

Robert Grimes couldn't be dead. Medical science certainly hadn't reached the point where they could regrow bones and I wasn't stuck in that time vortex for long enough for humanity to advance that significantly.

I took another sip of the amber medicine. My case files were a mess, laid out without order in front of me. Sometimes, mess helped. It focused the mind. Kind of. You saw the bigger picture and noticed connections not seen before.

I sucked on the cigarette and imbibed more of the alcohol.

I needed a fresh canvas.

With a sweep of my arm, papers plummeted to the floor, a mess that could wait for another day. I had a new mess to deal with.

I pulled out my SmartBoy, placed it on the now-empty desk and tapped along its edge. It beeped. The screen appeared, a blue outline, projected, floating above the fake wooden surface.

The projected screen trilled against my fingertips, haptic feedback strangely pleasant on my skin, as I typed across the desktop and found the obvious first target for my research: Professor Howard Lowe. The mystery of Robert Grimes would have to wait.

It was always a good start, to begin with the lowest common denominator, the missing person. I already had some background information on him; I knew he'd married my ex-wife for one. Secondly, he worked at Solaris University, studying something to do with a new power source and there was Big Business involved with his funding. Tribeca Corp, possibly, but I'd have to confirm that. Whoever it was, they certainly held a lot of sway. Robert had told me as much. There were plenty of eyes on Howard Lowe.

Not to mention Jill.

If I was being thorough, I had to check her out too, no matter my feelings toward her.

I stared at the screen; Jill's name was there, part of the bio on the University's site, listed as his spouse.

I tapped on the professor's research history and another page spun open in the air, a list of achievements as long as my arm. He was certainly productive. It was a wonder he even found time to bang my ex-wife.

Maybe it was finally time to accept she'd moved on. She had Howard, wherever he was, and I had Sam. Had. Goddammit.

I studied the screen. The most recent research project was labelled as something almost incomprehensible: Trans-capacitational Conduits and Parallel Sub-dimensional Acquisition Nodes. That was a mouthful. If Professor Lowe was working on something to do with a new power source, he needed to come up with a more user-friendly name.

It wasn't the first time he'd worked on Trans-capacitational Conduits either.

It seemed to take up the bulk of his research over the last decade; there were some other unrelated projects dotted in between but this was the most prominent. He was even working on it before he was employed by the University. A personal obsession of his, it seemed. There was some mention of him working in the private sector on the same project but the company he worked for had been redacted. My guess was Tribeca Corp.

I returned to the top of the list and tapped on his current research. I needed more information.

I was met with a wall of science.

Bloody hell, I needed a drink. I took a sip of my whisky and lit up a cigarette. It was going to take all my concentration to unravel this bullshit. Or at least, understand a fraction of it.

I sucked down the smoke and blew clouds through the transparent screen. There were a lot of long complicated words muddled between conjunctions and nouns; I had an inkling this was going to take all night. I considered, for a moment, moving onto an easier lead, but I'd still have to tackle this monstrosity at some point; may as well get it over with now.

The words blurred, either from the smoke or the alcohol or just my tired eyes. The room flickered; the lights were struggling. Maybe the professor's research was the key to fixing the power problems in the station, but I doubted it. There was too much potential for profit. The key to a successful investigation was always to follow the money. And there was plenty of that involved, almost definitely. All the companies interested in this research stood to gain from its success. So, why remove its most prominent person? To capitalise on the competition?

My mind was wandering; I wasn't focusing on the jumble of words before me. I had a plan and I needed at least a basic understanding of the text before I could head over to the University tomorrow. And, as far as anyone was concerned, Professor Howard Lowe wasn't missing. Police cover ups certainly had their uses.

The lights flickered again. There was a goddamned power outage on its way.

I took another swig from my glass.

The room went dark, leaving only the bluish light from my SmartBoy and its screen. The power cut prompted a top of my drink. I stubbed out the butt of my cigarette and reached for the bottle. What the hell; I unscrewed the cap and chugged straight from the source, sour goodness to quell the darkness.

I lit another cigarette to burn away the alcohol in my throat. The orange glow added a brief respite to the sapphire light laid out before me. This wasn't going to be good for my eyes, reading in this gloom. I blew smoke through the floating text.

The research was dry, drier than my love life was at the moment, especially after Sam had pretty much dumped my ass. Well, definitely dumped my ass. But he'd come around, I was sure of it. Eventually.

The cigarette crackled in my silent office and I took more of the whiskey into my soul; it warmed me, spreading throughout my chest and torso. The cold was creeping in from the lack of power and I was grateful that at least the shielding around Space Station Delta offered some protection against the soulless void outside. I'd have to make do until the reactor had charged the massive batteries at the centre of the station with enough electricity to get every running normally again.

I needed to piss.

I stood, a little woozy from booze and meds, and stumbled out of my chair. I took a drag on the cigarette; it's amber glow and the light of my SmartBoy were the only saviours to my staggering path to the bathroom. I reached the door and paused.

Something felt wrong. My instincts flared.

I don't know what made me second guess my own office, maybe the whiskey, maybe the meds, but something wasn't right. My instincts were screaming. I took a step back and studied the glass of the door. It held a shadow that was not my own, a dark reflection. My feelings when I'd returned to my office had been correct; there was an intruder. I shouldn't have ignored them. I took another step back and my cigarette crackled in my hand as it continued to burn away; it broke the silence.

Whoever was there, whoever was hiding in my bathroom, in my office, they'd made no sound. But I could feel them. Sense them. I could see their shadow.

"Shit!" My fingers burnt; the cigarette was spent. I threw the stub to the floor and looked up.

The door exploded open, the shadow barrelled toward me and I was knocked to the floor. A grey face, blue face, it was barren of features in the dark, I only saw a flash as I tumbled. My back hurt. My healing body rejected me.

He, or she, had escaped.

5. Chase

I jumped to my feet, ignoring the pain from my collision with the floor and the ache in my side, a reminder of the explosion. I grabbed my SmartBoy and ran into the darkness.

I raced along the corridor and burst through the door into the stairwell. I paused, listening, trying to hear any sound to indicate where the intruder had gone. The party in the apartment down the hall still thrummed distantly and I couldn't hear anything unusual through its beats. Without the blue of the screen, it had knocked itself off as I picked up my SmartBoy, my eyes strained in the gloom.

Something clicked, a door, at the bottom of the steps.

I continued my pursuit. The stairs almost caught my feet as I took them two at a time, almost leaping downwards after the intruder. I pummelled into the door and burst into the dark street. I stopped.

The moonlight above was just enough to see along the blackened streets. It was late. I must have sat at my desk longer than I thought. I looked up and down the street. It was empty. Except for me. And the shadows.

Something caught my eye, a glimpse of grey near an alley. Or white. It was hard to tell in this void, but it was familiar enough to spark my body into action.

The face of my intruder was my target, a pale circle in the dark. I ran. And the shadow fell further into the shadows around it. I sped along the pavement, it's uneven stones attempting to trip me as I ran, and focused on my prey, where my prey had been.

I skirted the corner and entered the alleyway. It was dark and gloom enveloped the enclosed space. There were high walls on either side, a narrow passage. Nowhere for the meagre light to go. Or the intruder.

I had them; they had nowhere to go.

My eyesight laboured against the gloom. The chase had gotten my heart pounding, adrenaline pumping away the alcohol, boosting my sobriety, numbing my injured body.

I'd never even noticed the silence until I felt the hum of the generators kicking back in. The lights surged, blinding me for a moment, and returned to their usual dimness.

I blinked, forcing my eyes to adjust to the meagre lighting, and saw my target; a figure in black with a white mask, blank and featureless, stood between the walls. He was ready to pounce.

I stood my ground. Somehow, the empty face seemed glad, despite the lack of eyes or mouth.

He ran at me and we grappled, wrestled. I could smell booze and cigarettes, sweat, but I didn't know if that was the stranger or me. My assailant was stronger, faster. His hand caught my arm and twisted. I cried out in pain. He was also a better fighter. Much better. A fist pummelled my side, my recent injury stung, and my legs went weak, and I crumbled. The masked man had winded me. Pain seared through my torso. I fought against it, forced my body to move, respond.

I reached and grabbed. I caught hold of his coat and the pull of his escape twisted me, dragging me back and straining my waist. I scraped across the paving stones, breathless from the blow to my injury. I turned onto my stomach and scrambled, struggled to my knees. A foot swung around, his shin caught me, hard as metal, and I felt wet pain on my face; I lost my grip, and with nose bloodied, blurring my vision, my prey kicked again. My head swung left and collided with the floor. More pain. Dizziness.

I rolled and avoided a heavy boot to my face; I heard the masked figure grunt in dissatisfaction. I avoided another stomp of his foot and somehow made it to my feet. I shoved him. He stumbled back.

My target was vulnerable; now was my chance.

My foot met his most valuable assets.

His gloved hands grasped between his legs and he dropped to his knees, letting out a cry of agony that I could only sympathise with. Something clattered to the floor, metallic, glimmering. I ignored it, for now. I swung and punched, fist smacking into the hard mask of my assailant. It was a mistake. Fuck.

My advantage was lost.

He came at me, one arm swinging, and I felt another blow to my head, dazing me. A kick was returned; I didn't sympathise as I fell to my knees.

I blinked through the water in my eyes. My face was wet, blood and tears on my skin, and my head hurt. So did my side. My vision cleared and I was left alone in the empty streets.

I reached for the object he'd dropped. Golden and rounded.

What?

My wedding ring?

Why in goddamned hell did he have my wedding ring? I quickly pocketed it.

I ran, running on instinct that my prey was heading in one direction and not another; I ran through the hurt in my torso and the hurt in my groin.

I caught sight of him; his coat whipped behind him as he ran. He was heading for the sector door. Sector Seven. Sleazy and rough, much like my own sector, but with its own particular flavour. It would be easy to lose the masked man in the throng of the decrepit pit that was the next Sector over.

He reached the large opening that led through and I wished that there was a way to trigger the safety door and trap him before he escaped me again. Only two things would do it. A big fire, which wasn't feasible. The other was damaging the dome. Impossible. I pushed my legs harder. He wasn't getting away this time.

The masked figure looked back.

A blank face.

"Stop!" I shouted; the impotence of this was lost on me at the time.

My prey kept running; he'd escaped from Sector Six and still had a head start on me. I followed, feeling the change in the air as I hit the sleazy streets. The screams and shouts of this Sector's occupants cried out in the distance; I was running into Hell, and not the bar.

The acrid perfumes of industry and narcotics tickled my senses and grew stronger as my journey deepened into the chasms of the neighbouring zone. Sector Seven was known for its poverty. And that attracted crime. Unlicensed industry chugged out archaic and forbidden fossil fuels; drug trade was rife. The cowardly cops rarely came here.

This wasn't my first time here, and it wouldn't be my last.

The streets were a narrow maze and tall, wobbly buildings had been erected haphazardly wherever they could fit. I still had sight of my prey. He ducked and weaved through the alleys and walls, and through the reprobates that had started to appear; Sector Seven didn't often sleep and most of its residents were the waking dead.

I had no idea who the masked assailant was or why he'd taken my wedding ring, but it was undoubtedly linked to the missing professor.

And he was fitter and faster. A better fighter too. I needed to come up with a plan to take him down if I ever caught up to him.

Then again, I might get lucky, something I was famously not known for.

People, drunk and high, were beginning to get denser between the walls of the buildings and it was becoming difficult to keep track of my intruder and avoid staggering idiots at the same time. I could hear music, getting louder as the streets busied; there must be a party going on ahead.

My path opened up into a plaza, I knew it well; it was one of the best places to get decent cheap whiskey when the detective business was slow, and I couldn't afford the premium stuff. Now, it bustled with alcoholics as they raved to the beat of heavy bass, celebrating the return of the power and lights. Sector Seven used any excuse for a party.

I couldn't lose the masked man in the crowds.

He merged into the dance, cavorting carcasses closing in on his path as he entered the throng. I rushed forward, trying to follow his route but I was soon consumed by the crowd, crushed by writhing drunken forms. I was going to lose him. I pushed on, forcing my way between elbows and knees jabbing me. I scanned the mob; the masked man was having just as much trouble getting through the horde of revellers as me. I just needed to clear a path. Somehow.

The music thumped and vibrated, so did the people. Drunk. High. I'd needed to make them scatter.

I squeezed between two rather amorous dancers, an understatement of their closeness, and I tried to keep my eyes focused on my target. He stood out. He wore his white mask and dark clothes while the frolicking mass of filth was a mix of colourful fabrics and neon jewellery. Still, there was a good chance he could elude me in the waves of rhythm that surrounded us. I needed to do something fast.

I pulled my notepad from my pocket.

I was probably going to regret this.

I gripped my lighter, my body was buffeted, pushed, bruised, bashed, and I attempted my plan to clear the way.

The paper caught.

"Fire!" I screamed through the cacophony. "Fire!"

It worked.

At least, at first.

The people dispersed, emptied around me, and a space opened. I ran forward; I moved into the swell of emptiness before me, my eyes focused on my target. The burning paper scattered the people and the crowd panicked, some screamed, but it was hard to notice over the beat and rhythm of the music that pervaded the sector and my concentration on the masked man.

I was going to get him.

I thought. I was so sure.

Dancers, confused and high, let me though without question.

And then, my plan flopped.

In the panic everything turned to chaos. The crowd, in its rush to escape the flames of my creation, closed its jaws on my passage. Teeth of elbows and knees shoved and prodded, worse than before. I was carried away, drawn back by the heaving mass. I was pulled further and further from the masked man.

My nostrils were filled with sweat and smoke. And disappointment.

My prey disappeared into the distance, and my body was hauled along by the horde; I tried to fight back, to push against the panicked people but it was useless.

I'd lost him.

Someone grabbed my arm. I was ripped from the crowd and pulled into an alley. I tripped and stumbled and, as I caught myself, I saw who'd saved me.

"Hello officers," I said, "fancy see you two here?"

6. Trouble

"Mr Gemini," said Detective Suede, "glad to see you're doing well. Recovered from your injuries, I see."

"More or less," I said. The detectives from the hospital, Suede and Johnson, in full uniform, stood side by side, blocking my pursuit back into the crowd.

"And already causing trouble."

"I don't know what you're talking about."

"Oh, really, Mr Gemini," said the police officer. He raised his eyebrows. "Just why are you here? Are you enjoying the party?"

"I'm a private and free citizen; I can go where I like."

"I suppose you're going to tell me you had nothing to do with that?" Detective Suede pointed to the rapidly shrinking clearing in the crowd; the flames were already nothing but embers and ash. "Lighting a fire in the open without a license is illegal you know?"

"Is it?" I tried to come across as incredulous as I could. "I hope you catch the perpetrator!" The dancing crowd resumed. As if nothing had happened.

"I don't suppose….?"

"I really don't know what you're talking about," I said as I thought about how useful this pair of morons might be. "You know, while you're here, you could help me with something. Someone broke into my office this evening."

"I think you need to report this through the proper channels, Mr Gemini."

"I thought telling a police officer would be the proper channels, detective."

"We're on a special case right now," said Detective Johnson. She was smirking, smirking like she was keeping some secret I wasn't supposed to know about. "We can't abandon it for a simple bit of breaking and entering."

"It might be related, you never know," I said. The crowd was beginning to thin as the ruckus moved deeper into Sector Seven. Silence followed the music as it escaped with the people. And my prey. "If you help me find my intruder, you'll find out if it is."

Detective Suede sighed. He reached into the pocket on his uniform and pulled out his SmartBoy. "I'll make a note of the incident," he said, opening up the screen. "I can't promise it'll go anywhere."

"That's it?"

The man nodded. "Johnson told you, we're busy."

I felt my eyes roll in my skull. "I'm not stupid, you know."

"Oh?"

"The reason you're here?"

"It's none of your business."

"I get the feeling you're following me."

"And why do you think we're following you?" said the detective. He lowered his SmartBoy and raised his eyebrows.

"Robert's death. I'm a suspect." I had other inklings for their appearance, but I wasn't going to reveal all my cards. "Apparently."

"Yes, you still haven't come to the station for questioning, Mr Gemini."

"I've been busy," I said, "and I only got out of the hospital today."

"You smell like you've just come out of a bar."

"It's a free world, station, whatever."

"Do you think that's wise after your accident?" said the female detective. "Alcohol shouldn't really be mixed with your painkillers and..."

Detective Suede motioned with his hand for her to quieten down. He cleared his throat. "Anyway, you said you needed some help with an intruder?"

"Yes." I wondered if they knew about my current case, the missing professor. "There was someone hiding in my bathroom." Of course, they knew about the case; the two detectives were keeping track of my movements. "He must've been there for hours; I was sat at my desk researching a case before I realised he was in there." They probably didn't know enough. "And I still need a piss."

Detective Suede turned his attention to his SmartBoy. "Can you give a description?"

"Not really," I said. "He was wearing a white mask, blank... and he was about my height and build, dressed in black."

"Useful." There was sarcasm in his voice.

"I chased him here and lost him in the crowd."

"And what exactly do you want us to do about it, Mr Gemini?" said the detective. "There's not really much to go on. You used to be a cop, right? You know we need a bit more than that to do anything. I mean, did they take anything?"

"No," I lied. Something told me not to tell them about the wedding ring. They might take it. As evidence. I wasn't going to let that happen.

"Listen," he said as he tapped along the screen, "I'll make a note of what you've told me. It'll be official. But until we know more, our hands are tied. You know how it is."

"He's got to be still in this Sector," I said. The partying revellers had all but moved on, the music and sweaty bodies as distant memory already. "Probably."

"You can make a full report when you visit us at the station to give your statement on the explosion in the bar."

"Is that all you're going to do?"

"Yes."

"In that case," I moved forward to try and squeeze past, but a uniformed arm stopped me, "if you'll excuse me; I've got things to do."

"Not quite yet," said Suede, "I told you we can take a full report on your masked man when you give your statement. Why not now? It's as good a time as any." His fist closed around my forearm. "And we can do that the easy way or…"

"Let me guess," I said, "the hard way." I sighed. "And I'm guessing you don't want to do it the hard way."

Detective Suede shook his head. Johnson had a stupid grin on her face.

"Fine." I gave in. "Let's go."

The large detective stepped out into the street and Johnson gestured for me to follow; she'd take up the rear. A copper sandwich. And I was the filling. This might be any normal person's wet dream. But not mine.

The three of us left the alley with my body moved along between the two cops. The drunken revellers had long moved on, the only evidence of its presence were the boozy detritus of broken bottles and trash.

My prey had escaped with them; he'd be long gone by now.

I was sure that wouldn't be the last I'd see of my intruder and I was certain he was intrinsically linked to my current case. I needed to get back to my office. Look for clues. Find out if the ring was the only thing he took, although I doubted it. He certainly wasn't there to harm me; he could've killed me if he'd wanted to. He could've done anything to me. Anytime. But he didn't. And he only attacked when I discovered him in the bathroom; he must've been there hours.

I still needed a piss.

My bladder pressed up against the waistband of my trousers and the belt tried to squeeze the urine from within.

As we moved along the street, I could make out the distant sounds of the chaotic party; it must be still happening. I thought the drunks and druggies of Sector Seven had dispersed, moved on; the streets had quietened when we left the alley, but we seemed to be heading toward continuing intoxicated festivity.

"This better not take too long," I said.

"Why? Do you need to find a lost cat?" said Suede. "Or do you need to get your rocks off by taking photos of couples in flagrante?"

"You might scoff but it's a hell of a lot cleaner than your line of work."

"Is that why you left the force?" said Johnson. She was behind me. "To perv on people having sex?"

"If only," I sighed. "An accident a few years ago ruined my life. There was no way I was going back to being a copper after that."

"You mean that time vortex thing?" she said. "I read something about that in your file."

"Johnson," warned Suede. "I'm sure Mr Gemini doesn't want to talk about it."

"I'm just interested in why he's no longer a cop," said the other officer.

"Why?" Suede seemed to be getting irritated by Johnson. "Are you thinking of a new vocation?"

We were getting closer to the party; it doesn't sound quite as fun as it should.

"I mean," said Johnson, "look at him; he isn't exactly rolling in money. He looks like a tramp."

"It's been a long day," I said. I didn't know why I was even bothering to explain myself. "Don't knock it 'til you've tried it," I quickly added with barely a hint of my embarrassment.

Detective Suede held out his arm, blocking the path through the streets. "I think we may need to take a different route to the station," he said.

"Trouble ahead?" I said. I couldn't contain my sarcasm. I could hear shouting ahead. Smashing glass. The sounds of violence. "It doesn't seem like the power party's going well."

"Power party?" Suede raised his eyebrows.

"You can't be that out of touch with the common people, surely?"

"It must be another term for breaking the law," said Johnson. As if on cue, a brick flew over her head and smashed into the wall behind her. "We better get out of here." She placed her hand on my shoulder and she gently nudged me to the left.

"That way will be safer," I said; I turned to the right. This could be my chance to escape. "We can cut around the main road and head to the transport station." I pointed down an alley.

"I'm sorry Mr Gemini," said Detective Suede, "but you'll forgive me if I don't trust you on this; you've been rather contrary in regard to coming to the station for questioning."

"Frankly, I'm shocked by that comment."

"It is what it is."

"So," I said, "I'm guessing you still want to go that way."

Suede nodded, and I felt Johnson nudge a little harder than before. I felt myself give in. Perhaps it was finally time to give my statement. Perhaps I should tell them about Robert's bones growing back?

Detective Suede took the lead again, followed by me, and then his partner. The noises of the oncoming riot were getting louder and closer. We were getting closer to the chaos. It seemed Johnson's suggestion was a better option than my own; I'd be able to flee my escorts in the coming commotion. I focused on the back of the detective in front of me while we walked. He wasn't as polished as I thought; he hadn't ironed his shirt. Hypocrite. They might mock my job and my appearance, but I caught many a philanderer in this guise. I'd even wooed Sam.

I needed to go make it up to him.

He'd forgive me.

I ran my fingers around the edge of the smooth metal in my pocket.

He always did.

As we walked through alleyways, I started to catch glimpses of people in the streets beyond. It was rowdy, loud. Frenzied. The population of Sector Seven were crazed tonight. It was to be expected; this sort of thing always followed a power outage, and the citizens of this part of the space station were particularly affected. Sectors Six and Seven were the poorest sectors, and while the more affluent parts of the station were always kept powered, we faced the brunt of the power problems. Sector Seven always became particularly riled by it; I was surprised Six didn't go the same way. Then again, Seven was a bigger hive of inequity and crime and its people were always angry.

Suede was leading us directly into a mass of rage.

Dangerous. But could be a way out.

We reached the end of our pathway; there was nowhere to go but into the crowd.

Suede turned to me. "Don't even think about causing any trouble," he said.

"Wouldn't dream of it." A finger jabbed in my back.

"He means it," said Johnson.

We entered the throng and my body was immediately buffeted by the riot; Suede's portly body was like a large rock in a riverbed and the water flowed around him and into me. It was painful. The bony appendages of the Sector Seven citizens hurt and the big detective's form did little to quell the flow; we were absorbed into the crowd.

If could only get ahead of the pair, then I could lose them just as the mysterious masked man had lost me. I could pin the two cops behind a wall of flesh.

I just had to wait for the right opportunity.

We were surrounded now, and a good distance from the alley we'd exited; there was no going back, only forward. I just needed something to happen, some sort of commotion within the commotion, a distraction to allow me to peel away. Suede kept looking back at me to make sure I was still there and I could feel Johnson's breath on my back. It stank; it was worse than the sweaty musk of the rioting crowd. People were shouting, getting worked up, and projectiles flew through the air, smashing into the buildings and roads.

This was probably the worst place the two cops could be. Even I knew better.

Civil disobedience surrounding two representations of the state.

And I was in the middle.

I still needed a piss. I contemplated just wetting myself there in the middle of the crowd, I mean, who would notice? The streets already smelt of shit.

The mass of humans was beginning to open a little, still packed, but less dense as we reached the widest part of the street. I felt the moment coming. Angry glances, death stares. All coming this way. Something was going to happen. Any minute now. Any second. A distraction. I didn't really care if the dozy pair got hurt; I could escape.

Detective Suede glanced back.

Now.

A drunk shouted an incomprehensible rant in our direction, something about pigs and anal, and a bottle crashed into the back of Suede's head.

The detective was pissed. His gun was in his hands almost as soon as the bottle bounced off his skull. He fired into the air and the waves of bodies parted.

That was a bad idea.

More projectiles collided with the detective and showered the surrounding street; they fortunately, missed my fragile, injured body. I stepped back. Johnson was still there; she placed her hand on my shoulder and shook her head. She didn't want to lose me. But she was going to lose control of this situation any minute now. Never provoke a riot. Never. Another mistake by these idiots. But it would be to my advantage.

Suede fired more rounds into the air and it only made things worse. An irked pedestrian rushed forward and tackled the cop; the two collapsed to the floor.

Johnson took action. "Stay here," she said. She rushed forward to untangle the mess in front of her.

Now was my chance.

I stepped back, absorbed by the crowds and was lost from my escorts; I left them to their foray.

I really needed to piss.

the final case of Jack Gemini

7. Respite

I walked back through the more familiar streets of Sector Six, keeping away from the main roads and streetlights; it was better that way. Who knew if Suede and Johnson had escaped the fracas and followed me?

I ducked into a narrow alley.

The streets of my home sector were quiet, as usual, but I looked around just to make sure before unzipping my fly and letting loose on the dirty streets. That little escapade had tired me out; my eyes were weary and unfocused in the dank, dark, and I struggled not to piss on my shoes.

I didn't succeed.

Goddamned waterproof shoes. Or, at least they used to be. Age and wear had caused my socks to become sodden with urine.

Fuck.

And the intruder, the masked man, had escaped me. He'd taken my wedding ring, but I didn't know why. It wasn't exactly an expensive ring; cops didn't earn a lot of money and neither did detectives so why had this been the thing he'd stolen? It didn't make sense. Just who was the masked man?

I stepped away from the puddle I'd created and leant against the opposite wall. It wasn't easy being a PI. Not with idiots like Suede and Johnson about. Any cop worth their salt would've taken the priority on a perp who'd trespassed on one of your murder suspects. Then again, I suppose I was a hostile witness; I wasn't exactly co-operating with them. Not yet anyway. I had my own plans, more important plans. Jill's case seemed to be tied into everything and I had no doubt it was tied to the death of Robert Grimes. The masked intruder was somehow involved. I was sure of it. It was all too convenient. My usual cases didn't involve such high stakes, and it was rare for a missing person case to link to murder; it was often a teenage runaway or a second spouse. Easy to find. And nothing too sinister. Usually.

I retrieved a cigarette from my pocket and lit up.

I needed to decide my next steps.

As much as I wanted to go back to my office and check that on the off chance that anything else had been taken, I couldn't just yet; I'd rather avoid the incompetent detectives, at least for a little bit, and they were bound to look for me there first. I needed some time to make some progress on my investigations, give myself some ammunition to push back against their questioning, gain the upper hand.

I sucked in the noxious fumes of the cigarette.

I needed somewhere safe, just for an hour or so.

This was going to be difficult.

Sam.

I needed to go to Sam's.

Granted, Suede and Johnson might try to find me there, but only after they'd checked my office, and with Hell just below Sam's apartment, there were plenty of escape routes; the history of Sam's bar was linked to banned alcohols and narcotics. Before Sam that is. Sort of. It's how I met him. He was working there when I uncovered the illegal operation. And now, he owned the bar. It was a long story, and I didn't have time to reflect on it.

I took another drag my cigarette.

I hoped Sam was no longer mad at me or, at least, he'd cooled enough so I could sweet talk him around. I also needed a shower. And surely, he'd let me borrow a change of clothes. If I could get him to forgive me I could get on with this case; I needed to head to the University and investigate Howard's lab.

I moved deeper into the alley and further away from the main streets. The morning was coming and the citizens of Sector Six were beginning to emerge from their downtrodden hovels and apartments. I'd need to take the back alleys to reach the bar.

I stepped through the stench of a homeless person huddled under a pile of dirty rags and hurried along behind the brick buildings; he, or she, was consumed by alcohol and, probably, drugs.

Sam hadn't meant the things he'd said. This wasn't the first time he'd dumped me, and it wouldn't be the last. He liked the excitement I gave him; the vicarious life of a P.I.

I was getting closer to the edge of the dome that encapsulated Space Station Delta. Of course, there was no way for the general layperson to get right up to; the lower section was kept securely behind thick walls and fences. But you could get close.

My office was near to the edge.

So was Sam's bar.

I flicked the spent filter to the ground; it was getting lighter now and the night's events were becoming more and more distant. Just out of the hospital, I still wasn't completely recovered from the explosion in the bar, and I dived straight into research. Pushing myself. Probably pushing too hard. Then there was the masked man, the intruder, and the chase. And that pair of annoying cops. My body and mind were exhausted; I really needed some sleep.

I ducked left and back toward the main street passing the overflowing bins of Hell and the broken bottles filling the alley.

Sam would be awake this early; he always had a delivery on a Tuesday morning. Wait, was it even Tuesday? I'd lost all track.

I reached the front of the building and hurried down the steps to the bar's entrance. The window was boarded up, a reminder of Robert's untimely and surprising death. And his miraculous regrown bones.

The bar looked completely shut down. No lights. No sound from within. He'd be there, Sam would be inside; he was a responsible man. Unlike myself. I tried the door, rattling the handle and pushing hard to try and get inside, but it was locked up pretty tight. Sam must've had the dodgy lock fixed. Unfortunately. Still, it was strange that the bar seemed all closed up; Sam was always awake early even on his free days.

"Sam?" I knocked on the doors. Maybe he'd seen me coming. "Sam?" I spoke a little louder this time and knocked again; I didn't want to draw attention to myself from the street, not with Suede and Johnson still after me. I knocked again and the silence continued to reply.

The damned man was ignoring me.

I'd need to break in. But not through the front door, that would be stupid, and I'd attract too many suspicious people. I'd go around the back; Sam had a bad habit of leaving his bedroom window open; it was on the third floor.

I took a few steps back toward the street, and carefully peeped over the pavement as I ascended just in case the two cops had the forethought to come look for me here at Sam's. There was no-one. No-one but dribs and drabs of people making their way to work; I'd certainly put too much trust in the duo's investigative skills. I headed back down the alley I'd approached from and made my way to the back of the apartment block above Hell.

Behind the tall building it was deader than the streets in front, danker and darker, despite the morning beginning to creep in. The dim lighting would help with what I needed to do. Breaking and entering. Sort of. It wasn't as if I hadn't been in Sam's apartment before. I even stayed over sometimes.

I eyed the fire escape above. I'd either need to climb onto something to reach the ladder, or, I needed to find something to pull the ladder to me. I looked around the dingy alley for anything that would help. Climbing was probably the easiest option. There were some empty boxes and crates a little distance from me, at least I hoped they were empty; it would be a pain in the ass to pull heavy boxes to where I needed them, especially with my side still aching from the spiroglass.

I gripped the edges of one of the larger boxes. It was heavy, just my luck, and I struggled to even shift it an inch. This wasn't going to work. There was no way I was going to move the crate close enough to the ladder without killing myself in the process. Maybe a smaller box was the answer; I could jump from there.

I picked my target and lifted it easily; it was about a quarter of my height and should provide just enough of a boost to reach the fire escape. This was going to hurt; my side still ached from the explosion and the strain was going to make it worse. I aimed the box just beneath where it needed to be and stepped atop. I looked up and took a deep breath.

I leapt.

One of my hands grazed the metal of the bottom rung; the other, caught. And slipped. I tumbled and crashed into the hard floor. Goddammit. It really fucking hurt. My torso had twisted and collided with the box which had slid under my feet, bounced against the wall and come between me and the ground. My head hit the concrete. And my shoulder was crushed beneath me.

I checked my pockets; it was still there, still safe.

I took a moment, just lying on the floor, before I climbed to my feet and tried again.

This time I was bit more successful; my hands grasped the bottom rung and I dangled like a marionette. The descending ladder wasn't descending as it should; it was stuck. My muscles strained; my side ached loudly. I really needed some time to recover, not only from the explosion, but from my fall, and I wasn't exactly at peak physical condition anyway.

I wiggled and shook through the strain in my overexerted muscles and tried to shake the ladder free. It was painful. But ultimately prosperous.

The ladder came crashing downward.

And so, did I.

It didn't hurt as much this time.

Once again, I climbed to my feet. I stretched to ease the aching all over my body and looked up at the newly opened route to Sam; the ladder was still on its rails, low enough for me to climb. I was going to make it up to him. Everything. Tell him I was ready to commit. Yes. But I needed to make sure he didn't find my wedding ring in my pocket. Or, at the very least, have a plausible excuse ready to hand.

Then I'd shower and get a fresh change of clothes.

I ascended the fire escape, the metal rattled as I climbed, and I soon reached my destination.

The window was ajar. I squeezed my fingers into the gap and pulled up; it was a little stiff, but the window shimmied up on its tracks until the opening was big enough to get myself into the apartment with relative ease.

"Sam?" I called out. The small bedroom hadn't changed since I'd last been here; it was still neat and organised. Just like Sam. A shelf of books was aligned in order of height, nothing out of place. A solitary lamp stood central to the bedside table and nothing cluttered the surfaces except what needed to be there; a hairbrush sat atop the chest of drawers, perpendicular to the edge. A humble mirror on the wall, straight. Even the bed was made.

Sam hated it when I stayed over; I always made a mess.

Talking of mess...

There were dark spots tracked along the normally immaculate white carpet leading into the living room.

I wished with all my heart that my instincts were wrong.

I knelt by the nearest splatter to get a closer look and my eyes caught sight of the body in the living room.

Goddammit.

No.

No, no, no.

A bloodied body despoiled the meticulous order.

No.

Sam was dead.

8. Succour

Eventually, I found myself in the one place Sam would never want me to go.

There was no going back to my office; my gut had told me to run, to get as far away as possible from the body. From Sam.

There'd been something familiar nagging at my brain.

I hadn't gone too far into Sam's apartment. I couldn't bring myself to. But I'd got close enough to see the green circle painted on his lifeless head.

A shiver had run down my spine.

I'd left immediately. I had to.

Sam was dead. This case was much more personal now. Robert's death, that could've been for any number of reasons but Sam, his only link to this case was me. Sam had died because of me. And what it worse was the mark on his head. The green circle.

Eight years ago, I'd chased a killer; I'd followed him into a science facility. And fallen into a time vortex. But there was something about this killer, this murderer, the one I'd chased.

He had a fetish for painting green circles on the heads of his victims.

Just like Sam.

Sam was dead. Sam was goddamned dead.

I didn't want to be alone. Not now. I needed someone. I needed her.

"What are you doing here?" said Jill. She looked furious. "You…" Her expression changed. "Wait. What's wrong?"

I couldn't hold it in anymore; all the sorrow, all the frustration, all the anger at losing Sam. I fell into her arms and felt my body melt away.

"Jack?" Her voice was softer than usual; I hadn't heard her speak like that in a long time. "Come inside. Quickly." She pulled me along, and I complied. "You shouldn't have come here."

My body felt weightless as she pulled me into the living room and dropped me onto the couch. Everything slumped.

"They've been watching the house," she said. "Stupid."

She moved away from me; I couldn't focus, and her form was nothing but a blur. She was the only person left I could go to. Jill placed something rounded and hard in my hand. A glass.

"Drink," she said. She pushed against my hand and moved the tumbler of amber liquid closer to my face. I could smell the sour liquid; it was strong. "Drink, goddammit."

I took a sip and the alcohol warmed my throat and chest. I downed the contents of the glass.

"Jack," said Jill. "Tell me what's going on. You look an absolute mess and you've risked Howard's life coming here. You were supposed to keep this whole damned thing quiet!"

"There wasn't anyone else." I felt my mind clearing, my body and my self-control coming through, back from the fuzz and into reality. It was risky coming here. Especially when I didn't know who to trust. "Jill," I said, "your case, your missing husband, this is getting bigger than both of us. It's about more than just a missing person. I can feel it."

"You're talking shit, Jack." She topped up my glass and moved over to the table to pour herself a glass. "You always talk shit."

"You're being watched, you said so yourself," I said. "Just because your husband disappeared. And that's just a small part of what seems to be going on."

"There were some big people involved," she said. She took a seat opposite me. "I told you there were a lot of people interested in what he was working on." She placed her glass on the table along with the opened bottle of whiskey. "Howard's work was important." She lit up a cigarette.

"Clearly." I finished off my drink and followed suit. The smoke filled my lungs like a comforting blanket. I sighed and picked up the bottle from the table. "This investigation is starting to cost a lot." I filled the glass to the rim.

85

Jull huffed. "So," she said, "you've come looking for more money? How dare you. We had an agreement."

"I'm not talking about money," I said. I took another swig of the amber drink. "Money can't bring people back from the dead."

"What? Are you saying Howard's dead?"

I shrugged. "I don't know. But that's not what I mean." I could feel myself choking up; I fought against it. I'd already shown this woman weakness by coming here and I didn't want to give her any more advantage over me. "I shouldn't have come here."

"That's something we can agree on," said Jill.

I stared up at the ceiling. She had a nice place. Clean. White. Perfect. No clutter. Simple and minimalist. Like his apartment. "Sam's dead," I said.

"Who's Sam?"

I glared at her. Of course, she wouldn't know who he was, who he was to me. What he meant to me. Heartless bitch didn't know what love was.

"Jack," she said. "Tell me what this has to do with Howard."

"I'm not sure. Not yet." I finished off another glass of whiskey before topping up my glass a third time. "But that makes two dead bodies since I started working on this case."

She grabbed the bottle of alcohol and pulled it closer to herself. "Did you just come here to drink me out of house and home?" said Jill. She took a sip of her own drink. "Two bodies?"

I nodded. "Robert Grimes. You remember him?"

"Robert's dead? When did that happen?"

"A couple of days ago," I said. My torso ached at the thought. "There was an explosion at a bar. Sam's bar. In Sector Six."

"Fuck."

"He came to warn me about you."

Jill sighed and took a look a long drag of her cigarette. "I should've known he'd do something like that. After all, he cared about you a great deal when you worked together."

I sipped at the whiskey, a sudden realisation washing over me. "You slept with him."

"It was a long time ago, Jack." She shook her head. "Anyway, it wasn't as if you were faithful either."

"No, I guess not."

She downed her drink and reached for the bottle. "Tell me what happened." The liquid spilt into the glass and a little overflowed onto the glass table. "I take it you were there."

I nodded. "He was worried about me getting involved with your case. He told me to keep away," I said. "And I saved his life. At least, I thought I did." I lifted my shirt to reveal the scars from my role in the explosion. "I covered him; I was hurt." I dropped the fabric and reached for my drink. I took a big gulp. "When I came to, I was told he was dead."

"Are you sure you saved him?"

"Yes, goddammit." I slammed my glass onto the table. "I don't know how it happened; they blamed the explosion, but I know I saved his life. I saved him. And now, he's dead." I let out a sigh. "This is getting out of hand already, Jill. And there something else, something odd. Scratch that. It's something goddamned insane. Robert still had his leg."

"What?"

"His leg, Jill."

"What about it?" She leant forward and covered my drink with her hand. "You've had too much; you're not making sense."

I slapped her hand out the way. "I haven't had anywhere near enough. Not after everything that's happened this week."

She glared at me.

"You're probably right." She'd think I was crazy if I told her the bones in Robert's leg had grown back.

"Tell me about Sam," said Jill. "You haven't told me who he is."

My heart winced when she said his name. "He owned the bar," I said.

"And?"

"And what?"

"You're not telling me everything."

I reached into my jacket and retrieved a cigarette. I lit up. "I was kinda seeing him," I said with the cigarette still between my lips. "On and off."

"Bullshit."

I took a deep drag of the cigarette and ignored her statement.

"You were in a relationship."

I kept quiet.

Jill laughed. "You're upset! Ha ha! You had feelings for this guy!"

"And you're a cold-hearted bitch."

She shrugged and leant back in her chair. Her face split into a smirk. "I can guarantee the reason you're so cut up about this Sam being dead is because you fucked something up and couldn't make amends."

"No."

"No?" The woman raised her eyebrows. "Really, Jack? How many years were we married? I think I know you pretty well."

I wished I hadn't brought up Sam. He was dead. Dead because of this stupid investigation. Dead. Dead because of Jill's missing husband. Dead. Dead because of me.

The woman stood and moved next to me. I felt her arm fall around my shoulder, the warmth of her body was comforting and her presence familiar. Her perfume triggered nostalgia.

"It was more than an on and off thing, wasn't it?" she said. "With him?"

"Who?"

"Sam. It was serious."

"Maybe." I took the final drags of my cigarette and stubbed out the remains in the ashtray on the table. "I suppose it could've been. At least, until just before he was killed."

Jill squeezed my shoulders. "I'm sorry."

I felt a scornful laugh escape my lips. "You know that's the first time I've ever heard you apologise."

"For fuck's sake Jack, I'm trying to help."

"I need more whiskey."

She huffed and uncoupled her grasp from around me; she strode over to a cabinet at the far side of the room. "Howard isn't a big drinker," she said as she opened the cabinet doors to reveal a multitude of glass bottles. "It's a good thing I am."

"You haven't changed a bit, have you?"

"Neither have you." She placed several bottles of booze on the table in front of me. "You're still an alcoholic asshole." She kept one bottle in her hand as she again sat beside me. She unscrewed the lid and drank straight from the bottle. "Here." She handed me the drink. "Drink."

I obliged. I wanted to get drunk. And forget.

Jill had other ideas. Similar ideas but not the same.

"Tell me about Sam," she said.

I shook my head as I necked a big swig from the bottle.

She placed her hand on my leg. "Tell me." Her touch was a consolation. "How long were you together?"

"I met him a few years back." I didn't mean to let slip but the alcohol was loosening my tongue. "It was just... fun."

"Ha," Jill said, "it always is with you." She leant in and kissed me on the cheek.

"Wait…" I pulled back, "what are you doing?"

She sidled closer, her breasts pressing against me. "We could both do with a little comfort."

"I… I just saw him dead," I said. "I don't know if…"

"Shut up." She tried to kiss me again and I moved further back; she followed. For some reason, my thoughts turned to the wedding ring in my pocket; she didn't know I had it. Jill kissed me. It felt good; I'd forgotten the sweetness of her lips, the taste of her, her warmth. I gave up, gave in, and returned her advances.

the final case of Jack Gemini

9. University

It had probably been a mistake last night, sleeping with Jill, and I felt guilty, but still, it had given me some respite from the events and spurred me onto the next lead of the case. I'd borrowed some clothes from Jill, well, from Howard, and headed out; I was sure he wouldn't mind if it led to finding him. Something he might take issue with, however, was the ring in my, his, pocket. And, of course, sleeping with his wife.

Hungover and tired from the early start, I approached the entrance to Solaris University. The campus took up about a quarter of Sector Three and only a small percentage, about a hundredth of its redbrick buildings were actually devoted to teaching; it was all about the research, state and business, but mainly business, sponsored research. Undoubtedly, it was a hive of corruption. Just like everywhere else.

But I wasn't here for that.

I took in the atmosphere. The main building was up ahead but I couldn't be too hasty and attract attention to myself. I walked slowly, like I belonged. It was all about appearances. And smells. It smelled nice here. Gone was the distinct undercurrent of urine and grime, excrement and industry. Here, in Sector Three, the air was filled with the aromas of nature. It was fresh and clean, with a bouquet of scents from the flowers growing along every pathway. Sector Three never had power problems and it seemed the air filtration worked at peak efficiency. This was how Sector Six should smell, if it weren't so neglected. Sector Three was clean and tidy, and so was its population. It was fortunate that I'd spent the night at Jill's; I certainly wouldn't have passed as anyone important in my normal Sector Six attire. I'd even had a shower this morning.

I reached the double-doored entrance to the reception. I took a deep breath and entered. It was time to play the part.

The reception was massive, which just went to show how important big corporations were to the university and its research. The tiled floor echoed under my shoes, Howard's shoes, which were a little on the small side; they squeezed my feet and I felt a little apprehensive about the deception I was about to commit. They didn't always work. But first impressions were important to any good ploy. I smiled, friendly and approachable. If this worked, on the first try, then I was good to go.

"Hello," I said to one of the pretty receptionists, obviously chosen for their looks. First impressions were good for universities too. He looked up from his screen. "My name is Flint MacDonald; I'm an inspector from…"

"Sign here," he said with the copious disdain of someone being disturbed from the most important work in the universe. "Visitors need to sign in." I glanced at what had occupied the man before I had so unjustly talked to him. Shopping online, it seemed. Underwear. Very important.

"I'm sorry, but…"

"Sign." He tapped his manicured fingers on a sheet of paper. "Sign here."

"Paper?" I said picking up a pen. "Archaic." I signed my name. The fake one.

"Traditional," said the receptionist. He didn't smile; he barely acknowledged my presence, barely looked at me at all. "All visitors must sign in. On paper."

"As I said, I'm here as an inspector for…"

"Don't care." He handed me a card attached to a lanyard. "You're signed in."

"I need…"

"You can go where you want." The pretty man pointed to the door to the left of the desk. He was plastic, hollow. He would not be a good lay. "You're signed in."

"Okay, but I…"

He shooed me, his hands wafting me away from his desk. "Off you go."

"But I…"

"The main doors are that way." He pointed to the door. "From there you can access most of the campus. Except for the research labs, you need security access for those."

"And how do I..."

"Excuse me, sir," the receptionist said, "but if you were here to see the research labs, you would have been given a level 2 access card from your company HR department before you arrived. As a member of the public, you have level 8 access. If you are here representing a company, please, either speak to your company representative or contact our PR team from our website."

Confused that my alter ego had been so readily dismissed, I thanked the beautiful and condescending man and headed to the door he pointed at. It was big and transparent, unlike the main doors, and surrounded by windows. I could see the gardens and buildings that lay beyond. The door, detecting my 'level 8' lanyard, swished open automatically as I approached.

Sector Three, and the University, actually had the budget to look respectable and habitable, unlike my home sector. It was clean. Tidy. It was a stark contrast to Sector Six.

I needed to be inconspicuous. But also look important and that I belonged there; someone with authority. It was a tall order. And I wasn't the greatest actor. Maybe it could be a wood through the trees kinda situation; I needed to look so arrogant and haughty that I was unintentionally ignored as 'one of us;' I mean, that how everyone else looked in Sector Three. Uptight and with a long hard stick jammed in their assholes. Constipated. Obviously, it was a symptom of rich living.

Part of me wanted the same. Minus the clogged bowels. Unfortunately, things had a habit of not changing; the rich stayed rich. Bastards.

I made my way across the wide-open and green square that made up the inner courtyard of the surrounding campus buildings. The outside was abundant with statues and fountains. Fountains. Damned fountains. The architect seemed to have a fetish for them; they were littered at every crossroads. Every water feature was different; I passed by one that seemed to portray a man doing something questionable with a dolphin. Another, a naked woman with a fish head spitting into another woman's mouth, at least it was a woman's head, on a fish body. Grotesque. The students and staff paid the saturated art no mind; they were obviously desensitised to the horror of the designer's depraved imagination.

It was oddly quiet; there were plenty of people moving through the campus but very little conversation. Everyone had an air of haughtiness and distraction as if they were too good for this place. Which was laughable because Solaris University was considered the best university out of all twenty-four space stations; there was literally nowhere better they could be. Myself, I gone to a University on Earth. They were all gone now. Earth didn't have much of anything these days.

But Sector Three was affluent and so was the University.

It didn't make sense that everyone was so damned miserable. It was true that people could find misery in anything.

I was closing in on one of the buildings and tried my best to keep a frown on my face as I approached. It wasn't hard. Not after...

I reached the doors and entered. I didn't know where I was going and needed to change that; I needed to find Professor Lowe's lab.

There was another reception desk ahead and this time there was only one person manning it; an older, larger woman with purple hair on her head and half-moon spectacles on the tip of her nose. Haughty. Pursed lips, purple to match. I pondered whether to flirt to get what I wanted from her, but she didn't really look the type to endure my advances. Flattery wouldn't get me anywhere, not this time.

I'd probably made a mistake sleeping with Jill.

I approached the fake wood barrier between me and my target.

"Hello," I said. I couldn't help but smile; I didn't know what came over me. "I wonder if you can help me?"

"Yes?" The frizz of lavender on her head seemed to have the same air of annoyance as her face. "What is it? Out with it."

"I'm looking for Professor Howard Lowe."

"He's not here."

"Oh?" I said. "Is he not? Perhaps you could direct me to his offices?"

"No."

"I was just wondering..."

"No," said the berated woman. "His work is highly classified; you need to be escorted by the professor himself."

"Well, perhaps you could just tell me where it is. For next time. When Howard..." an intentional slip of the tongue to infer I knew Jill's husband personally, "...I mean, when Professor Lowe is in attendance?" She might be more helpful if she smelt a connection between me and the missing scientist.

The receptionist shook her head; her lips pursed more than I thought possible.

I raised my eyebrows expectantly. "I'd like to make a good impression when I next see Howard."

"Absolutely not."

I sighed. "Can I take your name? Just so I can tell Howard how helpful you've been."

"Sir," she said, "Professor Lowe was the person who gave me the explicit instruction not to let anyone go to his lab unescorted so if you're unhappy with my..." she cleared her throat, "helpfulness, you can take it up with the professor himself. Now," she pointed to the screen in front of her, "if you don't mind, I have rather a lot of work to do."

"Then maybe you can direct me to the library instead?"

Her eyes rolled. "Straight out the doors, turn left at the Delartes Fountain, then follow the path to the building with the big sign that says 'library.'" A smile flashed briefly on her face, almost as if she knew she needed to be polite but didn't want it to last long enough to make an impression.

"Thank you." I returned the same breakneck smile. I had no idea what the Delartes Fountain was, and I didn't stick around to ask. The woman's face was thunderous, and there was no way I was getting caught in that storm. No way. She hadn't bought my story. If I could at least find out where the building was, there might be some way for me to get inside and put my detective skills to the test. There had to be some answers there. The library was the next best thing. It might even have a map.

I kept my eye out for the Delartes Fountain amongst the plethora of water features; I didn't even know what I was looking for. I might have to ask one of the miserable bastards lost out here with me.

I stopped at every statue along the path, pretended to look at something on my SmartBoy, and then surreptitiously looked to my left for the 'building with the big sign.' It didn't take too long to find what I was looking for and, as I discovered, the Delartes Fountain was a rather pornographic and explicit depiction of an anthropomorphised squid; it was a Lovecraftian nightmare of genitals and tentacles. What some people considered art truly baffled me.

The library loomed before me. It was an imposing building and I felt a little intimidated as I climbed the steps to the main entrance. If I couldn't find a map to Professor Lowe's lab then I had no idea what to look for. Perhaps, I could look at more of his research. Research that was online anyway.

This might end up being a wasted trip.

I'd come to Sector Three and Solaris University with a plan. And I'd been shot down as soon as I entered; I'd underestimated how stuck up everyone was. I'd naively thought the morons at reception would believe me to be some sort of inspector and show me everything. Goddammit. It was not going well. I needed to make the most of my time here and come up with another plan.

I headed straight to the stacks. It seemed digital copies hadn't supplanted paper quite yet; it was probably some sort of tradition to keep everything in physical form. I hated the smell of books, their musty aroma; I needed to find a terminal to access the library systems instead.

It must've been exam season; the library was particularly busy, and I struggled to find a free pod in the study area to use. It had been a long time since I went to college; it wasn't this fancy back then, back when Earth had schools. The pod was a little self-enclosed room within the bigger room. A seat. A table. And a terminal. All encased in a box just big enough for a person. Just what every studious student needed; a claustrophobic little cage to keep you on task without distractions. There was even a little timed lock to keep you trapped inside. Suffice to say, I did not use this feature.

I closed the door to my little 'study pod,' just for the privacy it provided, and sat in the seat. It wasn't particularly comfortable; not very conducive to concentration, but I made do. I didn't plan on staying here too long. Just get what I needed, if anything, and leave.

I tapped on the screen to start up the terminal and signed in as a guest. I was greeted with a 'Welcome to Solaris' video. Unskippable. Goddammit. It didn't tell me anything I didn't already know, and I tried to blank out the content, all twenty-five minutes of it, but the music was too pervasive and annoying; whichever sadist had made the artistic choices for this 'introduction' was certainly insane. The selection of instruments was bizarre and I was certain there was a kazoo in there somewhere.

Finally, the video ended, along with my belief in the human race. The screen displayed a glut of different icons. Most were entirely irrelevant. I scanned the mess in front of me for something useful. There was a link that just said 'campus.' I clicked it and prayed for a map to Lowe's lab.

Goddammit.

I was bombarded with mountains of icons overlayered on top of the others. Again, most were useless, but there were one or two that were of interest. 'Facilities;' that could hold a map to the lab. I tapped on the icon.

There was no map, at least, nothing that specifically told me where the Professor's lab was within the campus. It took over an hour to navigate the maze of information; the 'facilities,' option had spiralled into a mass of images and text files pointing the way to all the points of interest within the university. It was just nothing of interest to me. I'd forgotten how big this place was. And there were a lot of bathrooms hidden everywhere. On a positive note, there was a rather big section about the fountains and their history. I avoided it; there was no way I was going to revisit the cephalopodic nightmares in the courtyard.

I made my way back to the first screen and scoured the mass of words to find something else. It was another hour before I found something useful. And it still wasn't a map. The section I'd found was about the research carried out by the university over the years; it was far more comprehensive than the information I'd found at home using my SmartBoy. And I could filter the information by the lead researcher; in this case, Howard Lowe.

Trans-capacitational Conduits and Parallel Sub-dimensional Acquisition Nodes.

Howard's current project.

The text didn't offer anything comprehensible, at least, not to me; I didn't understand a lot of what was there. Big words. Strange acronyms. There was a lot of new information here and I didn't understand any of it.

I sighed and leant forward with my head in my hand and my elbow on the desk. I slipped and knocked the screen.

This was useless.

The text didn't even say where the lab was; I was never going to find it.

I needed a cigarette. Or some booze.

And then, something caught my eye.

An icon for Earth.

It was dated.

I tapped the link.

No. Professor Lowe's research led to Earth. And my accident.

I'd known that the work he was doing on Trans-capacitational Conduits was the same work he was doing eight years ago when he worked privately. I just didn't realise it was on Earth. In the same facility where I'd fallen into the time vortex.

Someone knocked on the study pod door.

I ignored it; I kept reading.

I needed to know why; I needed to know what involvement Professor Lowe had with my accident.

Another knock, more urgent.

I should've locked it because before I knew it, I was accosted by the very two police officers I'd successfully avoided last night.

"You're under arrest," said Detective Johnson, as I was dragged from the pod, "for the murder of Sam Whittle."

10a. Accident

8 years ago.

Earth.

Augustus Smith. The Emerald Killer. It wasn't my case, but I'd become involved. I was the nearest cop to the sighting. And I was alone. No partner. My old partner, Robert, had transferred to Space Station Delta. I didn't blame him, not after the operation; the bones in his leg had been decimated and a metal replacement was the only option. That was a nasty case. My new partner, on the other hand, I'd forgotten his name, I'd told him I needed to speak to an informant alone and like a good little newbie he'd complied. It was lie. I'd lied to my new partner. There'd been a good reason. Well, not a particularly good reason, but a reason. There were some things a cop had to do without the watchful eyes of a partner; it was something not wholly legal. And now I'd been dragged into something big.

Goddammit. I didn't know why I'd responded to the call; I could've just carried on with my side business and pretended I didn't hear it.

The problem was that I'd checked in with HQ about thirty minutes previous; they knew I was in the industrial district and if I hadn't responded it would have garnered nothing but suspicion. I didn't need the hassle. There were already rumours in the station that I was under investigation and I didn't want to add more fuel to the fire they were building.

I headed out with some haste. Smith had been seen in the area, clearly seen by the surveillance cameras and not by some fuzzy witness who may or may not have seen someone with the resemblance to the killer. It was a reckless move by Smith; from what I understood about the case, he was careful. Usually. Some of the more proficient and respectable detectives had been on the case for almost a year and had gotten no closer to catching the notorious killer. I'd tried to stay out of it, but I guess it was now my turn to get involved. The Emerald Killer had been the talk of the town, the talk of the station and the media for too long thanks to his unusual penchant for leaving a green circle on the foreheads of his victims. Every person, man, woman or other, had one thing in common: green eyes. It was Smith's creepy little fetish. Sicko.

I headed for the outskirts of the district; he'd been sighted near some large facility that mounted the boundary between the industrial sector and commercial. I didn't know much about it, only that HQ was very concerned that Smith had been seen near it.

I was going to be the good cop today.

I shouldn't even be chasing a known killer like Smith without back up, but here I was. Dammit, why did I choose now to do the right thing? Well, not the right thing, just the right thing to keep the station's eyes from my dodgy dealing; I could imagine the look on all their faces if I actually managed to catch Augustus Smith.

Me.

Doing my job.

Ha.

Ha. Ha.

I checked in with dispatch; back up was still an hour away. It was definitely all up to me to catch him. If I didn't, I didn't. No skin off my nose. I just had to try. And not get killed. My death was unlikely; I didn't have green eyes, but I could still end up as collateral damage.

The streets of the industrial district were quiet. They always were this time of night. Or morning. All I knew was that it was late and there was no-one about but hookers and druggies. And myself. And, of course, the killer.

I kept my eyes open, trying not to give the whores any attention, and scanned the streets for Smith. This was the street he'd been seen on and there didn't seem to be any sign of him now.

I might be too late.

It might be worth speaking to Candice. She was usually working around here and she owed me a favour or two.

I approached one of the rent boys to my left; he probably thought I was looking for some trade, but I never paid for my affairs. At least, not with money.

"Hey," I said.

"You looking for something, mister?" He fluttered his scabbed eyes at me. He did not look too healthy. There were blisters around his mouth too.

"Yeah, I'm looking for Candice. Is she about tonight?"

"Who's asking?"

"Tell her it's an old friend who needs a favour."

"Candice has a lot of friends," said the sex worker. "You smell like a cop." His breath was vile. "You could be anyone."

"Trust me," I said, "she knows me." I slipped him a couple of notes. Cash was on its way out, but it was always worth carrying a few credits worth. Cash was untraceable.

He nodded, subtly, but he understood. "I still need a name."

"Tell her it's Jack."

The rent boy moved a little back from me to put a message through on his SmartBoy. Candice wasn't the type to keep me waiting. Still, I was attracting some suspicious looks from the other whores and I tried to keep my eyes elsewhere; I didn't want to attract any of their pimps, at least, the pimps other than Candice. She had a pretty good relationship with the other 'self-employed' around this area and I certainly didn't want to get on the bad side of any of them. I was taking a chance by asking for Candice in the open like this; she usually liked to keep things private because she had a reputation to uphold. It didn't look good if she was seen cavorting with cops. Even ones like me. But she did owe me a lot of favours.

"She didn't sound happy," said the boy as he approached. "She didn't sound at all happy."

"I thought as much," I said.

He raised his eyebrows expectantly.

"Oh, right." I slipped him a few more notes.

He spoke in a whisper. "Meet her around the corner in the alley; she's waiting for you."

"This isn't going to be some sort of trap, is it?" I joked. "Where I turn the corner and get a beating?"

"That service costs more," he said with a wink. He smiled; it was awkward, and I got the feeling he was trying to be seductive. "If you're here again, come and look me up."

I reluctantly nodded and moved away. I headed for the alley with the full knowledge that the rent boy was watching my ass.

I turned the corner. There was no crowd of thugs waiting for me, just a fancy black car.

I recognised it immediately as one of Candice's collection; she had a lot of vehicles.

A bejewelled arm waved from a rear window and beckoned me closer. All the glass of the car was tinted, almost black, but I knew who waited within.

"Good evening, my queen," I said; I gave her an exaggerated bow. "And, how are you this lovely evening?"

"Cut the bullshit, Jack." She wore her usual thick wallpaper paste make-up; it didn't act as much of a disguise because she was never seen without it. "I think I know why you're here."

"Oh, really?"

She nodded. The plenitude of earrings and fascinators jangled loudly. "You here because of Augustus Smith."

"You've heard." It didn't surprise me; the painted whoremonger always knew what was going on where her girls and boys worked, even when she shouldn't. Candice always knew. I didn't know what or who her source was, but at a guess it was one of her high-profile johns.

"It seems once again our interests line up."

"Then you can owe me a favour another time," I said. "If this is for your benefit too."

"Oh, don't get me wrong, Jack," said Candice, "you get nothing in this life for free."

"Don't I know it."

The woman leant forward amidst a cacophony of rattling trinkets. "My little ones are in danger as long as he's around here; Marcus and Genevieve, two of my best, have green eyes, and I've had to take them off the streets for tonight. This Emerald Killer is costing me money."

"You and me, both," I replied. "I had to walk away from a very important deal for this shit."

"I expect you want to know where he is?"

"Why else would I come to you?"

"I thought it was for my sexy smile," she grinned through ruby lips. Her smile dropped. "I'm sure you can find a way for Smith to have an unfortunate accident."

"I'll let the law handle him," I said. "I'm not a killer."

"Morally bankrupt. Just push your morals a little more; you can do it. He's too dangerous and he'll just get caught up in the system; the law won't stop him, you know it won't."

"Tell me where he is."

She sighed. "He's hiding out in the Tribeca Corp building."

"The what?"

"Hand me your SmartBoy." She snatched it from my hand as soon as it left my pocket; she tapped in some directions and handed it back. "You really don't come this way often enough, as often as I'd like."

"I'll make more of an effort next time. It's hard. I've got to think about Jill."

Candice laughed. "Everyone knows you don't give a fuck about her; you've had more side pieces than a gun enthusiast."

"I'm trying."

"Don't say I didn't try to tell you otherwise," said the woman. She moved back into the darkened car and her arm ornaments faded from view; I could still hear them rattle. Like wind chimes.

I made my goodbyes and headed in the direction she'd laid out for me. She called out to me as the car's engine started up.

"Don't get yourself killed, Jack," she shouted.

Her vehicle disappeared and I was left alone with all the whores on the main street. I picked up my pace; Smith wouldn't stay there long. He was at the large facility he'd been seen near, the one straddling this sector and the next. Tribeca Corp. I didn't know too much about the company except that they were in the energy business. Power generation was very lucrative right now, especially with the looming energy crisis. It didn't help that most of the planet's population had abandoned this stinking place and emigrated to one of the space stations in orbit. I didn't blame them. Earth was turning into a garbage dump.

I reached the imposing building in very little time and quickly checked in with headquarters. Back-up was still thirty minutes away, a bullshit estimate; there was some sort of big accident on one of the highways keeping them busy. Augustus Smith, the Emerald Killer, did not seem to be their priority right now. It'd become mine.

Just my goddamned luck.

My next problem was finding a way in. The main entrance was fortified with big electric gates. A definite no-no. I started moving around to the right of the building looking for any indication there was a way in, or, indeed, any indication of where Smith had entered.

Inextricably, I found what I was looking for. It was almost too easy, almost as if the path had been laid out for me. I didn't like it. There was a ladder leaning against the wall, and at the top, a broken window.

Did Augustus Smith know someone was after him? Was this all a trap?

My instincts, worn away by years of incompetence, were telling me not to climb the ladder; they were telling me not to go after Smith. To wait for back up.

But how good would it look if I caught the notorious killer all on my lonesome?

This was a bad idea.

I didn't know what had come over me. I was never one to do things for the glory or adoration; I only did things for myself, to save my own hide. I was only doing this to keep the prying eyes of the precinct away from my... other dealings.

I stepped onto the ladder and climbed. It wasn't a high window, but it was tall enough to need assistance to reach it. I made sure my gun was loose in its holster; I wasn't taking any chances. I needed to be ready. Ready for whatever was waiting for me inside. The main lights were off and only the green safety lighting was providing any sort of illumination within. Smith had picked a good place to hide out. A quiet building in the middle of nowhere. It was surprising that there was no security about. Especially for a facility run by a big company. Cost-cutting always had its downsides.

Then again, it was probably all automated. They might have some of those fancy robot security guards with the broken A.I. They were popular amongst a lot of businesses, usually because they were so cheap. But they never worked as intended. More often than I'd like I'd be called out to a burglary only to discover the 'security' guard had arrested a mop. Or in one instance, half a dead cat.

And if Smith was inside, as Candice had told me, it was unlikely that the automated guard had gone anywhere near him.

I clambered through the window and emerged into a bathroom. My foot, conveniently, took a wash in the toilet bowl, and I was left with a sodden sock and trouser leg. That was great. At least the toilet was clean. I hoped. It was hard to tell in this light. There was certainly nothing solid floating around in the bowl, but the green lighting told me nothing of the water colour. I tried not to think about it as I moved from the stall to the door and into the hallway. I was probably going to end up leaving tracks along this flooring, the tracks of a one-legged man with a penchant for toilet water. Thankfully, I wasn't the one being tracked; I was the tracker. It seemed, that if Smith had come into the building the same way as me, he hadn't made the same mistake. There were no wet footprints leading away from the bathroom. I'd needed to decide which way to go.

I took a guess and headed left. I drew my gun in anticipation of a confrontation.

I could hear the distant grind and whir of machinery as I moved along the corridor. Something big and loud had been left running throughout the night and it was a mystery what it was; I didn't have a clue what Tribeca was doing in this facility. It was a large building and Smith could be anywhere. Maybe, if I could find the security control room, which managed the security cameras and guards, if the building had them, then I might be able to track down where the

Emerald Killer was hiding. I didn't have a schematic or map of this place. It was going to be easy to get lost and there was a strong chance I'd probably end up finding Smith before I even got close to finding the control room.

I tested one or two doors as I made my way along the corridor. Locked. Smith could be in any one of the rooms, but there was no way of forcing the locks quietly, and if I shot at them, I would alert him to my presence. All I could do is move forward. And be ready in case he jumped out from behind me.

The mechanical humming grew louder and as I reached the end of the corridor I was greeted by a set of large double doors. A metal gangway lay beyond, and, in the verdant light, I could see a large, warehouse-sized room filled with complicated and confusing machinery, and whatever it was, there was another hue to the illumination; an undulating white light emanated deeper inside.

If Smith was in there, it was going to be a nightmare finding him. The facility was large enough already, but this room was going to have a lot of nooks and crannies tucked between and behind the strange apparatus.

I opened one of them double doors slowly and slightly and slipped carefully through. I paused, scanned the room and looked for any sign of my quarry. Nothing. At least, nothing obvious. There was at least some evidence he'd been here; below the gangway the broken body of a robot security guard lay mangled with its servos and gears spilt across the floor. Smith could be close. I needed to be careful.

I took a few steps onto the gangway; there was nowhere else to go. Except backwards, and I wasn't going to do that. The metal grating creaked beneath my feet. The noise made me feel uneasy. An omen? Almost as if the squeaks and groans were warning me that the walkway was going to shift and collapse beneath me; I really didn't want to end up like the security guard.

I moved forward, gun in hand, expecting Smith to jump me. I kept looking, scanning, surveying the room below for the notorious killer, but there was no sign of him anywhere. Aside from evidence of his destruction, the robot. The equipment ground and whirred beneath my feet and the white glow I'd seen before I'd entered the chamber was revealed.

A large spinning vortex of white light was pinned between two pillars. It didn't quite look right. Like it wasn't there and was there at the same time. The light swirled and spiralled and it almost seemed as if it occupied more than the usual three dimensions. It was impossible. Mesmerising. It was difficult to keep my eyes off it.

I shook my head to clear its hypnotism from my vision. I needed to focus.

I tried to work out what I was seeing. The strange glowing whirlpool of light was being brewed by the machines around it, ignited from the tall pillars. The vortex was prominent, the whole purpose of this facility. Sparks trickled and caressed the surrounding contraptions, feeding the weird phenomenon. Or being fed by it.

I turned away from the entrancing light and continued along the gangway. I was beginning to feel uneasy. My instincts were screaming at me to run and I didn't know whether it was the effects of the odd vortex, radiation or whatever, or if the Emerald Killer was close.

There was another door ahead, and, to its left, a metal staircase leading down to the chamber floor.

I had a choice. Search this room. Or move on.

I ignored my gut and took the stairs. They were just as arthritic as the gangway, and I managed to get to the bottom without structural collapse and broken bones.

The machines were deafening, and the vibrations echoed through the soles of my feet; my ears hummed in synch with their sinister machinations. The battered robot was just ahead. I approached its metal corpse, making sure to scan the room for Smith as I neared. If he was here, he was doing a good job at remaining unseen.

The spinning illumination caught my attention again and I found myself turning toward it. I moved closer, bewitched by the spinning lights. A slope led down to the trench in which it filled, and I found myself getting near. This close, it seemed even more unreal, taking up more space than just this room. There seemed to be something drawing me closer. Pulling me. Inevitability? I wasn't sure. I didn't want to get any closer, but I couldn't keep my eyes from the spinning lights of the singularity before me.

I slipped and fell forward.

White filled my vision.

the final case of Jack Gemini

11. Transport

"You're free to go," said Suede. His portly frame filled the doorway.

"What?" I asked the detective. "What do you mean?"

"Apparently," he said, "someone high up has decided there's not enough evidence to keep you here."

"So," I stood up from the metal slab they'd called a bed, "you've kept me in here for how many hours, without questioning, or access to a lawyer, for nothing?"

"I still think you're guilty. So does Johnson. But that's not our decision. Unfortunately."

"Fortunate for me." I stood in front of Suede who continued to block the cell entrance. "Excuse me," I said.

The cop scowled at me. "You're one lucky fucker," he said. "Do me a favour, eh? Don't leave

Space Station Delta. I'm sure you'll be having another holiday with us soon enough."

"It's not likely; I didn't do it."

"That's what they all say," said Suede. "I, for one, think the evidence we had was enough. Your DNA was all over the apartment."

"Of course, it was," I said knowing full well that I hadn't stayed over Sam's in about two months. "We were sleeping together." The whole thing stank of a stitch-up. Just like this cell stank of piss. I needed to get out of here. "I want my stuff back."

Suede looked me up and down before ushering me into the hallway. I'd had a lot of time to think in that cell, it wasn't as if I was able to sleep, and I'd thought about my accident all those years ago. The disappearance of Howard Lowe, and the strange masked man, all linked back to that Tribeca Corp facility on Earth. Somehow. Did it have something to do with the Emerald Killer? I needed to do some research. I never did find out what happened to Augustus Smith after I fell into the time vortex.

Johnson was waiting at the desk where Suede led me. The pair never really seemed separate for very long and I wondered if there was more to their relationship than simply work partners. They shared a smile. There was definitely more there. More fool them. Mixing business and pleasure was always a bad idea. For other people. Obviously. Jill was an exception.

"I hope you haven't looked through my pictures," I said as I retrieved my SmartBoy. "There are a few risky ones." A nervous laugh escaped my mouth.

Of course, they'd looked through everything; I was, up until recently, a murder suspect.

Johnson only scowled in response. She returned my belt, tie and shoes. Anything I could've used to hang myself. Or attack someone with.

"Well," I said. I eagerly snatched up my wedding ring. I needed it safe. "I hope you find the real murderer."

Another scowl.

"Neither of us are happy about this," said Detective Suede. He handed me the rest of my stuff and I quickly pocketed it. "Just you wait until we've gathered more evidence. There's still the autopsy to go."

I shuddered. I didn't relish the thought of my lover being cut open and probed. I tried to push the feelings to the back of my brain; I had too much to deal with right now, but it left me a little nauseous. I had to solve Sam's murder. Why had the killer gone after Sam? He had nothing to do with Lowe's disappearance. Or my accident. The only link was me.

"You look guilty." The cop pushed me along the corridor; Johnson was following closely behind. "Don't get any ideas."

"Of what, exactly? You're letting me go!"

"For now."

"I won't be back," I said. I needed a drink. And a cigarette. "I already told you I didn't do it."

I was led through to the front reception and reached the doors leading out of the police station; the faux wood creaked open on automatic. Fancy. At least, it was fancy for Sector Six.

The doors slammed shut behind me and I considered what my next steps would be. First, I lit up a cigarette and took a deep drag. It felt good. They'd taken away my smokes while I was in the cell, so this was a welcome relief after all those hours locked in the small cell with only the smell of human waste for company.

I made my way to the bottom of the steps and onto the street; it was only five steps, but I'd smoked the whole cigarette by the time I reached the bottom. I tossed the butt.

I had no idea what time it was. I'd lost all track while locked up and it hadn't helped that I'd been unable to sleep. It was daytime, or sometime in the day. There were people about, some cars, and it looked just the same as the rest of Sector Six. Dirty. Messy. Poor. Most of my cases were domestic and it'd been a while since I'd last come to the police station. Not that it mattered. Someone had tried to frame me. I could guess who. And even then, I didn't have a name. Or a face. Just that mask. And I still didn't know how the masked man linked to everything else. Or why he took my wedding ring. At least, I'd managed to take it back.

And now, there was another mystery: who'd got me out of that cell? It was a mystery that I could tell would be answered shortly. Possibly by whoever was waiting for me.

In front of the police station, an autocar was parked.

And, flashing in LEDs on its passenger door, 'Jack Gemini.'

I wasn't a fan of these driverless vehicles, even less so when I didn't know who'd arranged them for me, but sometimes they were useful. Whoever it was, they were pretty rich. Or just anal about keeping their car clean; the black sheen was spotless, at least for now, and it probably wouldn't be long before the grime of Sector Six infected its surface.

I hesitated, but only for a moment. This was probably the only way I was going to get any answers. So far, I'd only gotten questions and it was about time this case started unravelling. I needed to catch a break.

I climbed inside.

I was beginning to get the feeling things were moving beyond my control.

It was comfy within. The black leather seating was warm and soft, and the dimly lit interior was perfect for sending my exhausted body to sleep. I fought against it; I didn't have time to sleep.

The autocar sped away. The windows were blacked out so it was difficult to see outside and the only thing I managed to make out was the distinctive green lights marking the entrance to the underground causeway connecting all the Sectors of the station; the driverless vehicle must be taking me somewhere important because, after all, Sector Six was almost at the bottom of the rung when it came to importance within Space Station Delta. I was curious about the identity of my mysterious and 'important' benefactor. The car descended beneath the sector.

I opened my SmartBoy; the light from its screen burned my eyes.

I typed up a quick message to Jill, just to keep her abreast of what had happened since I... since we... since yesterday. I spent too long wondering whether to end the message with a kiss.

"Jill," I wrote, "visit to Uni didn't go as planned. Arrested for Sam's murder but set free. Picked up in autocar by someone? On my way to somewhere, hopefully, to get answers."

I finally decided to end the message with "x."

It didn't send. The signal had gone. I sighed. Dammit. I tried again. And again. But still, the message didn't send. I'd send it later; I let the SmartBoy save the message in my drafts.

I placed the device next to my thigh and pulled out my cigarettes.

An alarm blared in my ears and the car spoke up in a robotic voice. "Smoking is not permitted. Smoking is not permitted."

Goddammit.

I returned the cigarettes to my pocket.

Damn autocar.

The alarm stopped.

I reopened the screen on my SmartBoy and tried, once again, to send the message to Jill. And again, it failed. I minimised the message and opened up the internet connection.

I tapped in a name: Augustus Smith. The Emerald Killer.

I found a database of news reports from just after the accident; there was very little about anything even vaguely orbital about my fall into the time vortex. I wasn't surprised. It was in the best interests of the company that owned the facility to keep things quiet and it would be a shocking indictment of the lax security protecting such a dangerous phenomenon.

I typed something else: Tribeca Corp.

Dammit. I couldn't find any mention of them in the database. I searched Tribeca Systems instead; I needed to stop getting the name muddled. Just an article about the company shutting down its operations on Earth and moving its headquarters to one of the stations. This station, Delta.

There was still no mention of my accident. Or Smith. There seemed to be no links between my accident, the Emerald Killer, or Tribeca Systems. Apart from the relocation. Perhaps that was their response to someone falling into an experimental time vortex.

I returned to my first query: Augustus Smith. There were several articles about his murder spree before the accident. But nothing after. No mention of him meeting justice, no mention of his death. Nothing. It was almost as if he disappeared from the face of the Earth. And, from space. There were one or two conspiracy theories about what had happened to him; one article even said he'd stolen the identity of a politician and run for President. I took it with a grain of salt; another called Smith an alien who'd returned to his home planet.

The only thing that tied into my accident was the coincidence that the Emerald Killer had disappeared around the same time.

This investigation was going nowhere; all I had so far was snippets and hints. Nothing concrete. Just my instincts. It was all tied together.

Howard Lowe.

Robert's death and the strange regrowth of his bones.

My accident.

The masked man.

Augustus Smith.

Sam's murder.

The autocar exited the underway and came to a halt outside a tall building in one of the more affluent Sectors.

Tribeca Systems.

The car had come to a stop outside the headquarters of Tribeca Systems.

Maybe, just maybe, all the separate threads were finally starting to knit together.

12. Deal

I took a moment to spark up and enjoy a cigarette. The car journey hadn't been long, but I needed to taste the smoky narcotics.

Tribeca Systems.

It was certainly an interesting turn of events that had brought me here.

Tribeca Systems Headquarters was an imposing towering structure of glass and metal, the tallest building in Sector Three. It was clean. Like the rest of the sector. And it was an architect's wet dream, like any building owned by Big Business, with stark corners and whiter than white metal fascias around the mirrored glass windows. Yes, it looked different to the other buildings. It stood out. On purpose. Unfortunately, other businesses had tried to do the same, and it made the surrounding area a mismatched parade of arrogant peacocks. Each one unique. Clean. This particular exhibitionist structure had the company's name, Tribeca Systems, emblazoned in a plain sans serif font with no capital letters, just above the large entranceway. Lack of letter design seemed to be this season's trend.

I blew out a plume of smoke and took a small pleasure in knowing I was somehow corrupting the air of this sanitary sector.

It was only yesterday that I was here, in Sector Three, snooping around Solaris University. That hadn't really worked out. But I was here now. And you'd think if Tribeca had wanted to speak to me then they could have saved me the trouble of getting arrested.

It was time to get some answers.

Finally.

Hopefully.

I flicked the stub to the floor and headed up the stone steps to the main entrance.

There was someone waiting for me; a large muscular man with a handsome face, possibly a security guard, and wearing a neat black suit, stood by the door with his arms crossed. His head followed my progress. It was hard to read his expression behind the dark glasses, but he did not look pleased; it was a requirement of his job to give the impression of a difficult bowel movement. He stepped toward me as I reached the top of the stairs. His hand sprung out to block me.

"If you'll come with me," said the security guard. His voice was deep, gruff. Sexy. "You're expected."

"I gathered that." I pointed to the autocar.

"This way."

I was led, almost pushed, through the main doors and across the main reception floor; my shoes, Howard's tight shoes, slipped a little on the polished tiles as I was moved hastily through the building. I felt the guard's strong hands on my back. He was certainly a good-looking man; I'd have to remember to get his number. For questioning. Obviously. He could crack my case wide open. Anytime.

We reached an elevator. It was just off to the side of the reception desk and pretty well hidden from the view of the front doors. A private elevator. The doors were golden and polished; it didn't look like it was used by the average worker in Tribeca Systems.

The security guard swiped a plain black card against a similarly coloured panel next to the elevator. A bell chimed and the doors slid open.

I felt my body pushed and bundled inside without a single word from the muscular man; my finely honed instincts told me that he wanted me to go in the elevator.

It was empty inside, apart from myself, and as the lift started on its journey upwards, I noticed there were no buttons or controls of any kind. The elevator had one destination. Two, if you included the ground floor where I'd been thrown in. The other destination was probably the top floor if I were to guess. Someone important would be waiting.

The elevator was slow. Deliberately so. Most lifts would reach their floors, no matter how high, in a matter of seconds; this one was taking its time. A stalling tactic. To make the elevator's occupants sweat.

Which meant I was seeing the CEO of Tribeca Systems. It had to be. Or, at least, someone almost as high up in the company. It made sense; it had to be someone with enough power and sway to get me out of the police station. And on further thought, the ones instructing the police to tail Jill, just as Robert had told me. Someone big.

I watched the number above the door slowly tick up. At least it smelled nice in here. And the golden walls looked perfect and unmarred, casting strange miscoloured reflections back at me. I looked rough and out of place. I hadn't really slept, and I was still wearing the same clothes I'd worn to the university. Howard's clothes. They'd been clean and tidy at first but now, not so much. I looked like a bum.

The doors pinged open. A large office, white and sparse, greeted my eyes and the surrounding windows let sunlight stream through from every angle. I exited the elevator and was greeted with the vistas of this height. Through the glass I could see most of the sector; it looked so small from up here and it seemed just as organised and clean despite the distance. I wondered what Sector Six looked like from above. A pile of shit most likely.

"Jack Gemini," said a voice. "It's good to finally meet you." I'd been too busy taking in the view that I hadn't noticed the woman standing at a desk at the far end of the room. She was bookish and attractive with an immaculate suit and smile. I was sure I'd seen her somewhere before.

"I suppose thanks are in order," I said. I flashed her a smile. She didn't react.

"Let's not rush into things; I haven't even introduced myself," she said. Her face was blank and unmoving; she was perfectly in control of what she was willing to show, what emotions she was willing to display. "My name is..."

"Dionne Bex," I said. "CEO of Tribeca Systems."

The woman's face cracked a grin, slight and understated. "Hmm, I'm surprised. There are not many people who even heard of me; I tend to keep myself out of the public eye."

"I'm a private eye; secrets are my bread and butter."

"Take a seat." She gestured to the chair opposite her desk. "We have a lot to discuss."

"I take it you got me out of jail." I didn't move.

The CEO nodded. She pointed to the chair again and I obliged; she waited for me to sit before she did the same.

"I didn't kill Sam Whittle," I said. I felt the need to impress this on the woman sat opposite despite knowing she'd got me out of the police station; the rich elite often had little in the way of scruples. "I was framed."

She shrugged. "We know," said Ms Bex. "However, it is unimportant." She removed her glasses and placed them on the desk. "Or rather, less important than what I need you to do for me."

"It's important to me."

The woman sighed. "Jack, Tribeca Systems has been keeping an eye on you since your ex-wife, Jill visited your office. We know you didn't do it."

"Then you could have prevented his murder."

"Who?"

"Sam's."

"No. And we were also unable to stop Robert Grime's getting killed before you ask. Although I suppose you're only concerned about Mr Whittle, given your relationship." She sat back. "We were tailing you, no-one else, and some things are beyond our control."

"It's all linked."

"Yes," she said. "It's the reason we need you."

"My case?"

"You're not the only person concerned with Professor Howard Lowe's disappearance."

"I gathered that," I said. "There's a lot of people interested in his research. A lot of suspects."

"Yes, but in our case, Tribeca Systems has a more personal investment; Professor Lowe was working for us."

"I know," I said. I reached for my cigarettes and placed one in my mouth. "At least, I thought as much. Jill told me someone big was funding his research."

"His work was sponsored by us." She leant forward and offered me a light. "We've had Professor Lowe on our payroll for the last decade."

I exhaled the smoke, taking pleasure in the brief burn in my lungs. "And what do you want from me?"

"We want you to continue with your case," she lit her own cigarette. "Find Howard Lowe. Dead or alive."

"Dead? That sounds rather final. And callous."
I took another drag. "Wouldn't you prefer he was
alive?"

"Yes, however, Professor Lowe is a significant
figure in the company; he's important to the very future
of power generation. We do not want another
company stealing our secrets."

"So, he'd be better off dead."

"As I said, it would be better if he was alive, but
if the worst happens, we'd rather know his fate either
way. No loose ends. We've invested a lot into
Howard's research, time and money, and we need to
keep control of the information surrounding his
disappearance. Tribeca Systems wants you to find him;
we'll reward you handsomely, provided you keep things
quiet."

"It seems no-one wants this out in the open."

"Just us," she said. "You'd be surprised the
lengths we've gone to already."

"Big Business really has no qualms about
anything, does it?"

"I guess not." Dionne removed a file from a
drawer. "And I should tell you now, Tribeca Systems is
not involved in anything illegal or morally spurious."
She pushed the document toward me. "Or will be
involved in anything illegal. Tribeca Systems knows
nothing about your investigation."

"What's this?"

"An NDA," she said. "We'd rather you keep this
whole thing quiet and out of the public eye."

"Why?"

"I'm not fond of a scandal, especially when it concerns this company." She stubbed out her cigarette. "Did you know we hold the power contract for Space Station Delta? As well as fifteen other stations. I'd like to keep it that way. Howard's research is the key to that. I don't want anything that will jeopardise that; scandals have a way of getting out of hand."

"Why me?"

"Convenience."

"Bullshit," I said. "You need a fall guy."

Ms Bex grinned, but only from her mouth; her eyes remained glassy and emotionless. "I can't deny the possibility hadn't crossed my mind."

"If anything went wrong, or this became public, you want me to take the rap."

"Did I mention you'll be handsomely rewarded? Very handsomely."

"I understand that. What do I get out of this? Apart from the reward. I mean, the investigation has hit a dead-end; I've got plenty of pieces, but I can't get it to fit together. Now, unless you can offer anything new, then I'm afraid I can't take you up on your offer."

"Then let me tell you this," said the CEO, "Professor Lowe's research into power has a connection to you."

"I know," I replied. "I just don't know exactly how; I know he worked at the facility, your facility, where I had my accident."

"He's been working on harnessing power from reality distortions."

"Reality distortions? Like time vortexes?"

She nodded. "Tribeca Systems had a facility. On Earth. Professor Lowe worked there. All his own research. Brilliant man. Everything was going well, he was getting somewhere, but because of your accident we had to shut the place down. The publicity wasn't good for business and we covered it up, most of the details. There's more to it than you know." The woman raised her eyebrows and smirked. "Do you want to know what we covered up?"

the final case of Jack Gemini

13. Revelations

"You haven't told me anything I don't already know," I said.

"Tribeca Systems is willing to give you all the files linked to the accident," said the CEO, "and everything we have on Howard Lowe."

"What's the catch?" I'd forgotten about my cigarette; a tower of ash had gathered on the end of the stub. It fell, dirtying the white carpet; the woman opposite didn't notice.

Dionne placed a small memory card on the desk and slid it toward me. "The information will delete itself in twenty-four hours. Well, twenty-four hours after you access the data."

"And?"

"It's everything, within reason, about the facility on Earth, Professor Lowe's research reports to HQ, everything about your accident; it was big news back then, at least, to those that knew the full story. You were famous." Her face cracked a slight grin before returning to its stiff façade. "Albeit a flash in the pan; your fifteen minutes."

"And if I say no?"

Dionne cleared her throat. She stood and walked to the window. Her back was to me when she spoke. "I should remind you that Tribeca Systems has been very helpful in regard to your arrest for the murder of Sam Whittle."

"Are you telling me I have no choice?"

The CEO turned to face me. "I'm not telling you anything."

"Really?" I said. "It sounds like you've got me over a barrel."

"No," said Ms Bex. "I'd just like you to remember who your friends are."

"And friends help each other, right?"

"Precisely." She strode to my side and towered over me. She was close, too close. I could smell her sweet perfume, feel her warmth. Her hand slipped along my shoulders. "Quid quo pro." She squeezed my tense muscles. Her other hand placed a pen in front of me. "All you need to do is sign the NDA." Her body lowered and her face was next to mine. "You won't regret it."

"I feel those words will come back to haunt me." I opened the file and scanned the document for anything troubling. "Still," I said, "I can always drink my regrets away." I picked up the pen and signed.

The CEO instantly took the document from me and moved back around to her position on the other side of the desk. It was as if that moment of closeness between us hadn't happened.

Ms Bex slid her glasses onto her nose. "You'll need to make your own way back to your office." She opened her SmartBoy, ignoring me, preoccupied with something on its screen. "Thank you for your assistance, Mr Gemini."

"You're… welcome." Now that I'd signed the NDA the atmosphere had turned cold. "Just so we're clear, I'm not an employee of Tribeca Systems."

"For the duration of this investigation consider yourself an independent contractor," she said. "And bear in mind, the files we have loaned you," she pointed to the memory card on the table, "contain sensitive information and company secrets."

"And they will delete themselves in twenty-four hours," I said. "Don't worry, I'm not going to sell the information to your rivals… despite Elongax being so successful at the moment."

"You mean Elongate?"

I nodded. "This," I picked up the card, "will only be used for the investigation."

"Hmph. Elongate wouldn't have any interest in it anyway; we bullied them out of the energy business a long time ago."

"They might want to get back into it."

She shook her head. "No," she said. "I would never allow it." She sighed. "Mr Gemini, as much as I appreciate your attempt at conversation, trying to get a rise out of me, don't you have things to do? I'm sure whatever is in those files will help you find Sam's killer."

"Don't you know what's in there?"

"I don't bother myself with the small details," said the CEO. "I know the summary; it's up to you to trawl through the minutiae." She stood and gestured to the golden elevator. "Tony will meet you on the ground floor and show you how to leave. Discreetly."

"Tony?"

"The guard who escorted you."

"Ah, yes, I remember." I felt a grin creep along my face. "He did a good job."

Dionne raised her eyebrows and reinforced her outstretched pose pointing to the exit. I took the hint and stood, remembering to take the memory card and stash it in my pocket.

Tony was waiting for me at the bottom of the elevator. As he led me to the back door, I kept an eye on his. I was deposited in an alleyway behind the building; it was just as clean and tidy as everything else with no debris or rubbish anywhere. I turned to get Tony's number, but I was greeted with a closed door. Damn.

I made my way into the streets and requested an autocar from my SmartBoy; the trip back to Sector Six would be expensive. Goddamnit. These Big Businesses didn't have any clue how difficult the average person had it; they could've at least given me some credits for the fare home. I picked the cheapest option; it would take a little longer to get back to the office but at least it wouldn't decimate my bank balance. And it would give me some time to start looking through the files.

I jumped in the autocar as soon as it arrived.

I sat back in the seat and tried to relax, just for a moment; I just needed some time to reset, rest. Some time to just get back to myself. I'd hardly slept, and I felt like I was running on fumes. Even the injury from bar seemed to be tired of healing, as if the scars were undoing themselves.

The case nagged at me.

I grabbed my SmartBoy and slid the memory card into the expansion slot. The screen flickered to life. Without the benefit of the underway's fast lane, I had plenty of time.

There were hundreds of files. And no organisation. It was almost as if the lovely Ms Dionne Bex didn't want me to find anything useful on this memory card; after all, the files would be gone in twenty-four hours. My gut screamed at me to look at the accident. But I wasn't going to find it easily. There was at least eight years' worth of documents on the memory card. I scrolled through the list. It was alphabetised but the file names were a garble of acronyms, shorthand and numbers. This was going to be messy. Most companies would usually have a policy on how employees had to name their files in order to keep things uniform and this set of files seems to be no different. I just had to crack the code. Business file names were usually archaic, and usually never updated since the company was established. There was one glimmer of hope. Rarely, and more so for Big Business, the policy document for file naming was included with any set of documents. I flicked through the list with haste; if it was there, it would be right at the bottom. I just needed to find it.

I looked up as the autocar chugged downwards and into the underway of the space station. Daylight vanished, and acidic yellow light took its place. I suddenly became aware of the strange smells sharing the cheap car with me. Or was it me? It stank of must and piss, I felt an urge to take a long hot shower for several hours; the police cell hadn't been the most hygienic and I'd slept in Howard's clothes.

I turned my attention back to my SmartBoy.

It would take much more than twenty-four hours to get through every file on the memory card. Perhaps Ms Bex had planned it that way. After all, she was only interested in what was best for Tribeca Corps and not what was best for Howard Lowe. Or me. It was all about profit. And the disappearance of a major player in their business would have an impact on their stocks. Eventually, when it all got out. It would only be about damage control. And the less I saw about their business the better. My brain was filling with conspiracy theories, ones that didn't make sense. Why would Dionne Bex even bother to give me these files unless she wanted me to use them? Why would she offer me a reward for finding Howard Lowe if she wasn't going to help? Perhaps this had something to do with the masked man? He was one of the only things I hadn't connected to this mess. And I'd only seen him the once. I checked my pocket; the ring was still there. Just who was he?

It all led back to the accident. And so, must the identity of the masked man.

I found what I was looking for; it had taken a lot of scrolling to get to the bottom of the list, but there it was. The policy on file names.

It was at times like these, during the most exciting part of an investigation, policy documents and file organisation, where whiskey was usually the most welcome. Then again, it was probably for the best that I didn't partake; I didn't want to dull the pleasure in trawling through masses of text.

I thought about lighting up. And whether this damned low budget autocar would even try to stop me.

The file naming system was confusing and unhelpful; each year had a different letter assigned, which, if someone with common sense had designed the system, should be at the start of every file name. But no. It was every fifth letter, which made it even more difficult to find what I was looking for.

Tribeca Systems and Dionne Bex weren't making this easy!

I flicked my finger and set the page scrolling before stopping it at random. Amongst the mess of documents, I found three files which all fell into the year of my accident. The first was just a list of employees. I skimmed through, just in case, but only Howard Lowe was familiar. The second was a little more interesting, and by interesting, I mean boring. It was a layman's description of the time vortex, possibly written by someone with a poor understanding of 'layman;' it was labelled as a 'starter pack for understanding the phenomenon.' I scanned over the text, trying to get my head around the verbose and longwinded language that the document had been cursed with. It seemed the strange vortex in the facility

143

on Earth wasn't everything it seemed, and this document had been made to explain everything to the investors at Tribeca Systems. This wasn't the first time the company had experimented with time vortexes. And probably not the last. Previous attempts to use the singularity for power generation had resulted in nothing but failure, with the power taken to create and maintain a vortex producing a minimal return. This one, the one I'd fallen into, was different; there was a vast amount of power created. I moved on. The next section contained a plethora of technical language, and despite the apparent the document's intended purpose to be easy to read, I found myself cross-eyed as I attempted to navigate it. The following section did contain something interesting. Me. Or rather, Subject A.

Despite the date of the document marking my initial accident it had been updated, there was information from the whole five years I was trapped.

I'd been very beneficial to Tribeca Systems, it seemed. Not that I'd seen any of that benefit. I'd been experimented on inside the phenomenon, tested to see how the vortex could be controlled and utilised to its maximum potential.

And then, something else, someone else.

Subject B.

I wasn't the only person to have an accident that day.

How in hell did I not know about this?

I continued.

The document went on to mention that Subject A, myself, had returned to his life after the vortex became unstable and collapsed. Subject B, however, had moved with the research lead; Subject B had been moved to Space Station Delta with Professor Lowe to continue the research.

But who was Subject B?

The masked man?

There had been only one other person in the facility when I'd had the accident.

Augustus Smith.

The Emerald Killer.

the final case of Jack Gemini

14. Return

The return to my office felt brief. I'd ignored the mess left by the police officers searching for any evidence of misdeeds, or perhaps it was my own mess; I didn't care. A decent night's sleep in my own bed was all I needed. That, along with a shower and a change of clothes, my own, the next morning.

I spent until noon trudging through the memory card given to me by Dionne Bex; there wasn't much time remaining before the files erased themselves and I made a conscious effort to take in as much as I could from the documents as I could. I looked for anything I could find about Subject B. I needed to confirm my suspicions.

What was unusual was that my identity was no secret in the documents; my name appeared time and time again. But Subject B's, nothing. All I'd found was some suggestion that Subject B had been experimented on after release from the vortex. He'd been transferred to Solaris University.

I knew what I had to do.

I found myself in front of the stern purple-haired receptionist once again; unfortunately, she was still the demonic gatekeeper to Professor Lowe's lab at Solaris University.

"You again," she hissed at me. Her eyes, peeping over her half-moon glasses, scanned and inspected me. "Have you come to murder me?" Her tone was dry and acidic.

"If I was, it would be self-defence," I said with a grin and a wink. "You could kill a man by looking that stunning." I felt myself wince internally; I'd considered this approach the last time I was here and decided against it but this time, I couldn't stop myself.

It was a mistake.

The receptionist took a slow intake of breath and her nostrils flared. She sighed. "Mr Gemini, yes, I know who you are," she said, "if you think that bullshit is going to work then you're mistaken, and frankly, I find you a disgusting waste of space. You caused quite the stir the other day and I'm really not in the mood for a murder suspect to trying to get in my knickers."

"Then how do you feel about an innocent man in your knickers? I was released without charge."

Her eyes rolled. I didn't think anyone could manage a ten-eighty-degree spin with their eyes but, this woman, could; it was amazing really. Her lips pursed and she sighed, again. "You're disgusting."

"But charming?" I raised my eyebrows. I really didn't know why I couldn't stop myself flirting even though I knew this strategy was a dead-end; maybe it was the rare decent night's sleep.

"No." The receptionist remained expressionless.

I leant forward and rested my elbows on the desk. "Have you ever considered getting your eyes fixed? I mean, your eyes really are quite beautiful." They weren't; the bloodshot and yellowed spheres glared back at me. I really didn't know why I was continuing with this flattery and I'd known it wasn't going to work before I'd started, but I just hadn't been able to resist, to at least try. It was time to stop the act. I cleared my throat and stepped back from the desk. "I really need to get into Professor Lowe's lab," I said. "It's important."

"No," she said as she peered over her glasses. "I've told you before." A varnished fingernail, purple and cracked, targeted at my face, jabbed at the air. "Do you want me call campus security? Or the police?"

"I don't think you want that kind of drama," I said. I placed my hand over hers and lowered her pointed finger to the desk. "I'm sure Tribeca Corp wouldn't want anything in the press."

"What has that got to do with anything?" The receptionist pulled her hand away. "And it's Tribeca Systems. Not Corp."

"You and I both know they're funding Professor Lowe's research. Would it surprise you know they're also funding me?"

"Yes." Her face wrinkled in disgust. "I don't believe you."

"I was in a very important meeting with Tribeca's CEO yesterday." I lowered my voice and leaned in closer. "You've obviously heard about Professor Lowe's disappearance? Yes?"

The woman nodded; her expression remained stern. "You shouldn't know anything about that."

"And doesn't that tell you something?" I said. "I obviously know more than I should; it stands to reason that Tribeca Systems have me in their employ." I felt my gut telling me that this logic wouldn't stand up to much. I was right.

"Or maybe you're the one behind the good professor's disappearance?"

I forced a laugh; she was becoming tiresome. "Do you seriously believe that I would just stroll in here if I'd kidnapped that poor man?" I laughed again. "Doesn't that seem a little stupid?""

"Mr Gemini," said the receptionist. Her lips pursed. "I hope you're not calling me stupid."

"Certainly not. I'm just trying to reason with you."

Her eyebrow raised; her face was a portrait of disgust. "I am not stupid." She spoke calmly and measured; she removed her glasses and sighed. "You need to leave." The receptionist leaned to the side to look at something, someone behind me. "There are far more important people for me to talk to."

I followed her gaze to find out what had caught her attention; the coming storm strode toward the desk in a shapely white dress and red lipstick. A lot had happened since I'd last seen Jill. It was only a day or two ago when we'd slept together and I'd since been arrested, bailed out and chewed up by the big machine that was Tribeca. And yet, I'd do it all again. Just for her.

Guilt crept up my spine. I would've done the same for Sam.

My torso stung, still not recovered from the explosion, and I nodded to the approaching woman.

Jill face greeted me with a hint of a smile tainting the edges of her lips. She glared at the stern receptionist. "Hello," she said to the woman on the other side of the desk.

"Mrs Lowe," came the reply, "I had no idea you were coming in today. Does the Dean know you're here?"

"No, and I'd like to keep it that way." She shot me a quick glance. "I need to get into my husband's labs."

The purple-haired receptionist cleared her throat and gave me the evil eye. "I hope you're not going to take this..."

"Yes," interrupted Jill, "yes I will be taking Jack with me. And before you say anything more, and I know you're dying to, you should be well to remember the influence I have in this University and it would be beneficial to yourself to bear in mind exactly what I am able to do. Understood?"

"Yes, ma'am." The stern-faced woman returned her half-moon glasses to their usual place on her pointed nose and she tapped something on her SmartBoy. "I'll open up access for yourself. And your... er... gentleman friend."

"I really hope you're not insinuating anything?"

"No, ma'am." The woman was avoiding making eye contact with Jill; I fought against a giggle. Her SmartBoy trilled a happy little tune. "Access is granted." She turned to me. "The doors will open for you as long as you remain in proximity to Mrs Lowe."

"Come along, Jack," said Jill. She grabbed my arm and pulled me along. "We haven't got long."

We traversed the length of the desk and through a door at the far side; the suspicious eyes of the receptionist never left my view and her bloodshot orbs followed our every step until we were out of sight.

"It's good seeing you again," I said.

Silence. We were alone in an empty corridor.

"I've missed you," I said.

"Don't mistake the other night for anything other than it was."

"And what was it? I thought it was two people enjoying each other's company. Reconnecting."

"It was nostalgia," she said. "And we both used each other to feel better. Myself, because of Howard's disappearance. You, because of Sam."

"Bullshit," I said. "That might've been how it started but..."

"I'm in love with Howard, Jack." She brought us to a halt outside another door. It was labelled with Professor Lowe's name. "I'm not in love with you."

"Who said love had anything to do with it? Not that it didn't. I just..."

"I'm only here for one reason," said Jill. "You need to find my husband. Ms Bex told me to take you inside his labs; she told me you were going to have trouble getting in on your own."

"You've spoken to Ms Bex?"

She nodded. The door opened and I followed my ex-wife inside. "She and I are close."

"Oh, really?" The room we'd entered was on office of sorts, basic and plain, without many of the usual decorations befitting someone of status; something you'd usually see in a high-profile professor's office.

"Yes. We often brunch together."

"And what?" I said. A couple of doors led out and big glass windows displayed a larger room beyond. It was all very familiar, like I'd been here before. "Discuss nefarious plans together? Come up with different ways to torture me? Fuck?"

"No." Jill sighed. "Not everything is about you, you know."

I walked over a filing cabinet and opened the top drawer. "It might as well be." I flipped through the folders.

"And what's that supposed to mean?"

I slammed the cabinet closed; there was nothing of interest there. "I think you're still in love me."

My ex-wife laughed. "You've got to be kidding me, Jack; you're deluded." She moved toward the window and looked out. "This is where he does his experiments," she said. "I don't understand any of it."

I came up to her side and looked out with her. It was dark beyond the glass, the lights were off, and I could just about make out large pieces of machinery and equipment that looked more and more familiar to me; it was almost as if I'd been here before.

"It might hold a clue to his disappearance," I said. I turned and looked at her while she stared into the gloom. "Did you know?"

"Did I know what?"

"That Howard Lowe was working at the facility where I had my accident."

Jill was silent.

"You did, didn't you?"

More silence.

"Oh my God, Jill, my accident is the whole reason you met Howard isn't it?"

She still said nothing; her expression remained unreadable.

"Goddammit!" I walked away from her and headed for the door out into the main facility. The door swung open with ease. "Jill, I can't believe you! I can't believe you would do something like that!" The flickered to life as I entered and headed down the steps toward the machines; I didn't care if she was following me or not. "You know what, Jill? This is exactly the sort of thing you would do. I can't believe I keep falling for your bullshit!" I reached the bottom of the stairs and stopped.

"I don't know why you're surprised," came her voice from behind me. "It's not like it's any different to what I used to get up to, what you used to get up to, while we were married; it's just this time, I fell in love. With him. With Howard."

I couldn't reply to her; this time I was the one staying silent. I just didn't know what to say to her, didn't know what to say to heal the hurt in my chest. I thought I had her back; I thought everything was getting back to the way it was. Sam had seemed such a distant memory the other night and having him missing from my heart hadn't seemed so painful whilst I had her in my arms. She had to feel the same. Had to. I still had the ring. My wedding ring. Our wedding ring. I'd kept it all these years and it had to mean something.

My memory clicked, why this all looked so familiar.

"I've been here before," I said.

"Impossible."

"Well," I said, "not exactly here. It should look very familiar to you though." I looked up. "Although, this place does have a different ceiling to the other one so to you, it must look very different."

"What?"

"I don't imagine you got a full view while you were on your back."

"Cheap jibes," said Jill as she approached from behind. "They're really not a good look on you; you used to be far wittier, Jack." She handed me a cigarette.

"This looks almost the same as Howard's facility on Earth."

The woman offered me a light and I took it with little hesitation. "What in Hell are you talking about?"

"Where I had my accident? Where you met your husband?" I walked forward and pointed to each machine. "These were on Earth. And that one. That one, too." Two pillars stood, tall and imposing, wired to the machines, a space where the time vortex would be. "This whole place is almost a replica of eight years ago."

"I don't really remember," said Jill. She blew out some smoke from her own cigarette. "I never really paid any attention to Howard's work."

I took a drag of my own smoke. "And see that there?" I pointed to an empty space between two large machines, machines that held the most familiarity. "That's where the vortex was; that's where I was trapped. Howard is trying to recreate the accident. Or at least, the time vortex."

"And why would he be doing that?"

"There was something unusual about it. That's according to the documents I got from your brunch buddy."

"The time vortex? Unusual? They're not exactly common."

"This one was different." I exhaled more smoke. "There's got to be more here. More files. More information about Howard's research." I paused and turned to Jill. I needed to tell her. "I wasn't the only person trapped in that time vortex."

"What?"

"Someone else was trapped."

"What do you mean?"

"I was Subject A," I said. "But there was someone else."

"Who?"

"I don't know." I inhaled more narcotics. "I'm hoping there'll be more information here on 'Subject B.' There wasn't anything much on the memory card Ms Bex kindly loaned me."

"I surprised she was trying to help at all; she's rather business orientated."

"She wants your husband found too. It makes sense, businesswise." I stubbed on the remains of my cigarette on a wall, marring the paint. "Do you know where he kept his important documents?"

"No," she said. She flicked her used butt to the floor. "But there is a little space under the stairs where I'd often find him when I brought him lunch."

We got to work. We found two cabinets and some paperwork; the truly important information would be stored electronically but there had to be something, some clue, amongst the scraps and shreds strewn throughout the storage and desks. I wanted to find anything that could tell me the identity of the Subject B, anything that would point to his whereabouts. Was he the masked man? Was Subject B Augustus Smith, the Emerald Killer? Something in this room had to have the answer.

"I didn't mean to happen like that," said Jill. "It just did."

"What?" I chucked a pile of useless papers to the floor.

"Howard and I."

I sighed. "You can't help who you love."

"No, no, I guess not."

"Did you ever love me, Jill?"

"I've told you before." She handed me a document. It was just a purchase order for a piece of equipment; it didn't seem particularly relevant, but I put it to one side. Just in case. "We weren't, aren't, good for each other."

"You didn't object the other night. You even started it."

"I guess I did," said Jill. "Listen, Jack, I miss Howard; I miss having contact with him. You were just a substitute."

"I don't believe you."

"And what about Sam? His body's barely cold and you're jumping into the sack with anyone."

"Not just anyone," I said. "And Sam would've understood. He wouldn't have liked it, but he'd have understood. He'd have forgiven me."

"Ah, so you treated him the same way you treated me." She placed her hand on my shoulder. "Why didn't you tell me about him when I first came to your office?"

I shrugged. "I guess my feelings for you stopped me."

Her hand broke contact. "Are you serious? You can't be serious? We haven't been together since before your accident. We both moved on."

"You moved on," I said. "I didn't. Life's not been quite the same since the accident. I feel lost, Jill. Lost without you. Out of place. You can't tell me you don't feel the same?"

"I don't." She turned back to the cabinet she was looking through, and, with her back to me, continued rifling.

"I don't believe you."

"You can believe whatever you want, Jack; it doesn't make it any less true."

"You still love me."

"As a friend."

"We're not friends, Jill," I said. "We're more than that."

"You're deluding yourself."

"You're the one deluding yourself, Jill; we're meant to be."

"And what about Sam?"

"What about him?" My heart felt crushed, but I knew she could help heal the heartache. "You'd have liked him. But me and him... it wasn't anything like you and me. Just like I know you and Howard, as much as you love him, it's nothing like what we had, what we have."

"We don't have anything, Jack. Not anymore."

"We could have it again; it's never too late. I love you Jill." I thought about showing her the ring. It burned in my pocket. "And I know you still love me. You can't deny it."

"Our relationship was toxic," she said. "And anyway, Howard is still alive; I know it."

"It doesn't change our feelings for one another."

She paused. The swish of papers decrescendoed to a halt. "It may have been a mistake coming to you about Howard's disappearance."

"I disagree," I replied. "This whole thing would've dragged me in anyway; it's all linked to the accident."

She faced me and grabbed my arm. "Jack, I can't be with you."

"Yes, you can."

"No."

"We can be together, Jill. I'm still going to find Howard. We can be together, and we'll sort everything else out later." I grabbed her arm, opposing hers holding me. "Admit you love me. Admit it, Jill. Admit it."

"Oh, Jack..."

Somehow, we'd moved closer and I could feel her breath against my lips. Her breathing was fast. So was mine. Hearts beating, rapid and in synch.

"Jill..." I whispered.

"I know," she said.

She stepped in closer and her lips pressed against mine. We kissed. Passionately. I didn't know for how long but the whole world slunk away. We were alone. Just me and Jill. Her and me. I could smell her flowery perfume, her scent. I didn't want this moment to end.

But it did.

She stepped back and let go of my arm. "Jack, I..." Her eyes were moist, and on the verge of tears. She stepped further away. "This was a mistake."

"Jill, it wasn't," I said. "You can't tell me that didn't feel right?"

"I'm sorry." She hurried away and headed to the stairs. "I can't"

BANG!

The explosive blow echoed through the room and filled my ears. It had come from nowhere. A gunshot. Someone had shot her. Shot Jill. Her body fell. Blood splattered. Time slowed.

I rushed to her side, grabbed her hand.

Her last words, as she slipped away, as her body slumped, as her lifeblood filled my hands, reddened the white of her dress, I swore I'd never forget them.

She'd told me she loved me.

the final case of Jack Gemini

15. Lost

It was at least another day before I made it back to my office. Suede and Johnson had kept me in questioning longer than was necessary and seemed to purposely take pleasure in it. Damned bastards. They hadn't cared that this was the second lover I'd lost this week.

I needed to see this to the end.

For her.

I hadn't seen the killer.

Just a shadow.

It didn't make sense.

If Subject B really was behind this, if he really was the masked man, the Emerald Killer, then why hadn't he stuck to his sick fetish. Jill didn't have green eyes. The killer had just shot and run. And no green circle.

It didn't add up.

Either the killer had changed, which was unlikely, or there was someone else, an accomplice. Perhaps, even, there was no link between Subject B and the masked man; the masked man might have a completely separate agenda. Not that I knew what either agenda was. And having a second suspect only complicated things.

It seemed the closer I got, the deeper and deeper the mystery and the more questions that remained unanswered.

There'd only been death so far.

Three.

First, there'd been Robert Grimes, my former partner. His death had been odd; I'd saved his life by taking some spiroglass to the torso and that hadn't been good enough. Somehow, Robert had still died.

I took my feet down off the desk and reached for the drawer. I needed some whiskey and a smoke.

Robert's death hadn't been anything like Sam's. He'd died, apparently, of injuries from the explosion. And no green circle on his head.

I filled my glass to the brim.

Robert didn't have green eyes.

I took a sip of the amber liquid and swung my feet back on the desk. I leant back.

Robert's death, Robert's murder. What was the motive? A message, a warning to me? Or something else?

And there was the question of Robert's missing metal leg. His miraculous regrown bones.

I slid a cigarette from its case in my pocket.

Sam. Poor Sam.

I hadn't been fair to Sam, and he'd paid the price. He'd been murdered while I chased the masked man, if not just before. This added to my suspicions of a second suspect. Who was in Sam's apartment while I ran through Sector Seven? Or had it happened just before? Had the masked man distracted me while Sam was killed?

I lit up and took a long drag.

Sam's death had not been pleasant. A set up? I don't know. Misdirection? Maybe. The clues pointing to the Emerald Killer, Augustus Smith, seemed a little convenient. And it didn't add up with the circumstances around the other two deaths. The only link was the fact that Smith was the whole reason I'd ended up in the time vortex accident in the first place. He'd been the only other person in the facility at the time.

I gulped some more alcohol and took another drag of my cigarette.

Sam hadn't done anything to deserve his fate; his only crime hadn't been loving me. And he'd been murdered. Not me. It should've been me. I hadn't loved him enough. Sam had died waiting for me to love him back.

I emptied the glass.

It still didn't make sense.

Nothing did in this case.

And I still didn't know exactly what this had to do with my accident. Only that there was a definite link;

Howard Lowe had been in charge when I fell into the vortex and now, he was married to my ex-wife.

I took a final drag of my cigarette, lit another and topped up my glass with whiskey.

Jill was dead.

Shot.

Murdered.

I placed the wedding ring on the desk and stared at the golden metal; I tried to catch my reflection in its gleaming surface.

She'd died in my arms and her blood remained still soaked in the fabric of my shirt. I hadn't had a chance to change; Suede and Johnson hadn't let me. And despite them thinking I was innocent, they'd taken the chance to grill me while I was down, a chance to torture me.

Jill had been out of my life for years; I'd barely communicated with her since the accident and then she'd stormed into my life only to be taken away so quickly. It had felt like we hadn't been apart. Nothing had changed. I still loved her, still pined for her. And she'd felt the same. Oh yes, there were complications; Jill was married to Howard Lowe, the man I was looking for, but it might have worked, given the chance.

It was too late now.

Jill was dead.

Taken from me.

I blew some smoke over the top of my glass and watched it dance along the amber liquid.

I needed to get to the end of this investigation.

I picked up the ring and peered through it.

I needed closure.

I dropped the gold band back on the desk, and it rattled against the fake wood. Damned thing. I don't know why I still had it. I sipped some of the smoky liquid and took another drag on the cigarette. I needed to numb the pain.

And this case, this investigation, was going nowhere fast.

I was at a loss.

There'd been nothing in Professor Lowe's lab, at least not anything readily apparent. And it wasn't as if I could go back there anymore. Not without Jill.

And the memory card, the one from Ms Dionne Bex, CEO of Tribeca Corp, had erased itself. It was useless. The only real information I'd been able to gather from it, in the brief time I'd managed to look through the plethora of documents, was that someone else had suffered the same fate as me.

Subject B.

I'd been lucky with those files. There'd been no way I would've been able to look over every single file on that memory card. Ms Bex must've known that.

I finished off the second glass of whiskey and slammed the glass on the desk.

Goddammit, I needed to catch a break.

I stood up and walked to the window. The void beyond the glass, where my translucent replica resided, welcomed me but it wasn't as if having my blood boil in the vacuum of space was going to provide any answers.

Perhaps if I'd lived in a more affluent sector on Space Station Delta, I'd have reached this conclusion sooner.

There was one place left I could get answers.

It was the only place I could go.

I needed to go back where this all began. Where this all began for me, at least.

Earth.

16. Found

Space elevators were always cramped, stuffy and they stank of sweat and piss like any decent public transport. I hated them. And they convulsed like an overdosed junkie whenever the circular carriage was fired to and from the planet below.

It had been a few years since the last time I'd needed to take one and generally I avoided their use; I preferred my current orbital home. I knew the station pretty well, knew its people and intricacies, it's quirks. Earth was nothing but a distant memory. Unrecognisable to the planet I'd known before the accident. It had been a shithole before, but now...

I offered my ticket to the inspector and slipped inside the constrictive carriage. It wasn't exactly small inside, but whichever corporation operated the elevator had decided to utilise as much space as possible in order to squeeze as many people inside the space as they could. And, as I'd anticipated, it stank. It was a very unique eau du parfum. It wasn't particularly pleasant. Sweat and urine, as expected, but also a damp musk that permeated the sharp aroma of ammonia.

I took a seat near the outer edge with my back to the exterior wall. I hadn't checked it before I sat, and I was slightly concerned that I may have sat in... something. It was too late now; I needed to accept my fate. And I hoped that the soggy patch on the underside of my thigh, firstly, would dry out before I reached the planet, and secondly, was a substance that was neither toxic nor unsanitary. It might've been both.

The lights flickered.

The cabin was filling up fast; the seat to my right had already been taken by a rather grubby man whose scent complimented the musky atmosphere and the rest of cabin was congesting with persons of a similar calibre. I probably didn't stand out. Not while I wore my scruffy suit and grubby hat.

The lights flickered again.

It seemed we were heading for another power cut.

I tried to get comfortable in the cramped seat, a misshapen bucket that had been constructed with the very best in ergonomic design. I hoped the power would go before the descent started; there was nothing more terrifying to me than plummeting to the Earth's surface in total darkness. And my trousers were still damp with the mysterious moisture.

I wished I could light up a cigarette, but it was expressly forbidden in such an enclosed space as the elevator carriage.

Damn.

And then, the inevitable happened.

The lights flickered and expired.

The darkness was not comforting. Neither was the smell. People say that your other senses become heightened when you lose your sight, and that may be true, but I wished it wasn't. And it wasn't just the smell that was detestable, it was the noise generated by my neighbour's stomach growling and percolating, and likely adding to the aroma in the carriage.

The carriage soon begun to fill with chatter and the trills of SmartBoy games; silence gave way and even the man's bubbling belly was thankfully drowned out.

Someone, a lady from the cabin grew, placed a few battery-powered lanterns on the floor which provided some, if not totally inadequate, illumination to the dreary chamber.

The empty seat to my left became occupied. A latecomer. It was lucky for him that the power had cut out or they'd be waiting another couple of hours for the next one. I closed my eyes and pretended to be asleep; my brief glimpse of the bearded man hadn't left a savoury impression and the dim light hadn't helped.

"Excuse me?" It was the new arrival. I didn't respond. "Excuse me, Mr Gemini?" He tapped my arm and I continued to ignore him. "Mr Gemini?"

Wait. How did he know my name?

I opened my eyes.

"Mr Gemini? Jack?" The man had a long thick beard encasing nearly his entire face, thick glasses that were almost comical, and a wide brimmed hat.

"Do I know you?"

"Sort of," said the stranger. "We haven't met. At least, not until now. But you do know who I am. Just as I know who you are." He cleared his throat and his voice became but a whisper. "We have a common acquaintance: Jill."

I suddenly realised the man was wearing a fake beard, and had it not been for the poor light within the carriage it would have been immediately noticeable. It was bad. It seemed a University tenure did not come with any expertise in creating a credible disguise.

"Jill…" I said.

He placed his hand on my arm. "I know."

The gloom concealed my watery eyes and I did my best to hide it from my voice. "I'm sorry," I said. "I…"

"We can grieve… I can grieve later," said Professor Lowe. "There are more important things to worry about."

"You're life's in danger."

He nodded. "I've been in hiding since I found out his plan."

"Who's plan?"

"I assume Ms Bex has been in touch? Did she tell you that you weren't the only person to fall into the parallel sub-dimensional conduit?"

"I'm sorry? The what?"

"The phenomenon? At my Earth facility?"

"She didn't exactly tell me," I said. "You mean Subject B?"

"Yes, Subject B. Or Subject A. It depends on which way you measure it." He sighed. "It doesn't matter; what matters is that its time I put a stop to it."

"Just who is Subject B? His name wasn't mentioned in any of the paperwork," I said. I leaned in a little closer. "Jill, she came to me; she wanted me to find you."

"And you have."

"But this all has something to do with my accident?" Part of me wanted the power to come back and shed some light on Howard Lowe. "I don't understand."

"You don't have to understand," he said. "We just need to stop him."

"But who is he?"

The man's face scrunched up in thought and he sighed. "It wouldn't be a good idea for you to find out. And I don't know what would happen if you did. It certainly wouldn't be healthy for you, for your mind, your mental health."

"Trust me, my mental health is the least of my worries," I said. "My brain already feels like it's been put through a blender this past week. You need to tell me who he is; I can help. It will help. If I knew who he was I could track him down."

"If you keep on your current course, you'll get all the answers you need."

"Tell me," I said, "tell me is it Augustus Smith?"

"If you like," said the professor. "If that's what will keep you sane, Mr Gemini. The important thing is we need to act quickly. Subject B is close to putting his plans into action and we need to be ready to stop him."

"I don't understand why you won't tell me his identity."

"It's better you don't know," he said. "And I do worry I did the right thing all those years ago but only one of you was needed for testing. I guess he got the short straw."

"If you can call it that." I needed a cigarette. "And you still haven't told me who 'he' is." A drink. "You're being deliberately obtuse." A strong drink.

"It was intentional, you know."

"What was? You, making this whole thing more difficult?"

"The vortex." He seemed to be avoiding my questions on purpose. "At the time, it was the peak of dimensional engineering. Not that it was perfect. It was going to solve humankind's power problem once and for all. But the accident put a stop to all that."

"Tribeca shut it down."

Lowe nodded. "It was all covered up. The last thing they wanted was a scandal about a highly dangerous and experimental sub-dimensional conduit created in a lab funded by them. Especially one which claimed two victims."

"Did they move you to the University?" The power outage was still ongoing, and I was thankful; I needed to keep Professor Lowe close. I'd found him, or rather, he'd found me. Maybe I could put on end to this whole sorry saga if I could just convince him to tell me who the mysterious Subject B really was, and what it had to do with me.

"Solaris University was more discrete," he said. "For Subject B's tests. I needed to work out just how you both managed to survive and it would've been problematic had I taken you both. Suffice to say, I think I would've preferred you. He has... the other one saw a little too much of my work and as soon as I knew what he was up to, I had to disappear. He would've killed me."

"Why didn't you take Jill with you?" I asked. "Didn't you at least think to tell her where you were going?"

"Subject B would never harm her. Never."

"Are you sure?"

"I am positively certain," said the professor.

So, that meant Subject B wasn't behind her death. There was definitely a second suspect.

"I couldn't tell her where I was going," continued Lowe. "He would've sweet talked her into telling him where I was." He adjusted his bread. "Now, bear in mind, before I tell you more, I haven't recreated the original experiment quite yet, just smaller, more manageable versions. The first experiment, yours, could've gone much, much worse."

"What do you mean, worse? It's already ruined my life, and someone else's."

"If you don't have my expertise, the parallel sub-dimensional conduit has the potential to collapse and create a black hole; it would, undoubtedly, crush billions."

"That's one way to solve the energy crisis."

"This is not a joke, Mr Gemini!" He cleared his throat and took a slow breath. "I've the advantage of hindsight. He does not. Or rather, he doesn't care. I've spent the last eight years carefully refining my research to prevent such a thing. It might've happened all those years ago." He pointed a finger in my face. "It didn't. You're lucky to even be alive."

The lights flickered on and for a brief moment, I could see the professor's face, before the power cut again, and the gloom returned. He was terrified.

"He's going to recreate the vortex," he continued. "And he'll end up killing everyone."

"Why?" I said. "What possible reason does he have for doing such a thing?"

Professor Lowe shrugged. I could tell he was lying; he broke eye contact and looked to the side. He knew exactly why.

I grabbed his arm. "You need to tell me everything. Enough of this bullshit. You need to tell me who is and why!"

He shook himself loose and stood. He leant forward and whispered. "Careful, Mr Gemini, you don't want to make a scene," he said. "You could put both our lives in danger." He straightened up and adjusted his raggedy hat. "Good luck."

And with that, he left the carriage.

I thought about giving chase, but it would be foolish; short of torture there was no way I was getting anything more out of that stubborn bastard. I'd found him and he wasn't worth the reward. And I was certain he'd turn up again.

He'd left me with a lot to think about.

Too much.

My brain swirled as the power returned and my body was catapulted toward Earth.

the final case of Jack Gemini

17. Facility

The straps of the respirator's mask cut deep into my cheeks and it was hard to breathe through the plastic filter.

I despised Earth, what it had become.

It was a dump, a used and abused, spoiled and sloppy dump of a planet. A blemish on the entire solar system. Not that the space stations were much better; twenty-four orbital habitats which only had the added bonus of air filtration. When it worked. Earth's atmosphere was polluted and thick and I could even smell the wretched aroma through my respirator. It was difficult to see through the thick and muddy grime permeating everything. Even the autocar I'd used had struggled to get from the elevator station to the facility; it had been slow, but I was here now. At last.

Eight years was a long time.

The building looked almost the same, if a little older, decrepit and somewhat blurry in the dirty fog. Abandoned. Empty. I couldn't see any lights in the windows, not that it was easy to see even from this close.

I approached the imposing structure; I wondered if the ladder on the right side of the building was still there after all this time. Probably not. It had been almost a decade since I last went inside. Still, it would be convenient. The front entrance, through the thick air, seemed to be just as well fortified as in the past. But it was worth a shot; it might be the only way in. I took a few steps forward. The building was neglected. It seemed doubtful that Tribeca Systems had kept the budget running to protect an empty shell and I hoped for very little resistance to gaining access to the interior.

The big electric gates, once closed, were open and I reached the main double doors with ease. Through the fog I could see a crooked metal plate with Tribeca Systems' logo and name imprinted on it. It was dirty and stained, forsaken, much like the rest of the planet. The interior of the building would undoubtedly be the same.

I paused. Moving through the sludge of the atmosphere was exhausting; not only was it hard to breath but not being able to see more than a foot in front of my face was beginning to take a strain on my eyes. And my brain. This might all be a waste of time; I didn't even know if I was going to find anything in the facility. There may be nothing. And my trip to this shithole of a planet could be pointless. If this place didn't have anything, any information, any clues, then my investigation would officially be at a dead end.

It all just seemed to be one obstacle after another. And one loss after another.

I leant back against the wall, the muscles in my torso aching from sucking air through the respirator, tucked in from the winds, and considered lighting up.

I stretched my weary muscles and reached for the door handle.

I didn't have time to grieve. Not yet. Not until this case was over. I had to know how this was all connected. How it all connected up to me. And my accident. It was personal. This case had a vendetta against me.

The door, to my surprise, was unlocked. Luck? I doubted it. It was too convenient.

And what was even more convenient was the illumination within. The lights were on; they'd looked off, on the approach. Damn atmosphere. But there was no green emergency lighting, no dinge. Lights. I could just about make out the distant sound of machinery. Even the air filtration was running; the interior was clear of the brown smog.

Someone was here.

The facility wasn't as abandoned as I'd thought.

Was I walking into a trap?

And if so, who had set it? The masked man? The Emerald Killer? Subject B? Or was it all just a strange coincidence, taunting my paranoid brain?

There was only one way to find out.

I stepped inside and closed the door behind me. I dragged the respirator from my mouth, let it dangle from the elasticated straps. And sucked in the reasonably fresh air of the facility; my face felt sore from the apparatus, but each breath replenished me just a little. A cigarette would help. I lit up and polluted the empty reception area safe with the understanding that the filters would suck away any evidence of my habit and prevent my detection. I hoped. It was a little risky, but I needed it, needed to taste the smoky clouds of narcotics within my lungs, especially after my long trek through the grubby and toxic whore-less streets of the industrial district of planet dammit Earth.

I looked around. The building was certainly not in regular use by Tribeca, despite the apparent occupied status; the reception was in a state of disrepair, with soft chairs torn and tattered, scattered across the tiled floor, and broken and cracked display screens behind the desk. It was still in a better state than the rest of the planet outside.

I stubbed out the dregs of my cigarette on the wall and moved further into the room.

There were two doors on either side of the desk, windows showing further illumination beyond. I was at a loss. The signage had long gone the way of the dinosaurs and I had no clue which way to head; using the traditional entrance on my second visit to the Tribeca facility may have been a mistake and I contemplated, briefly, returning to the smog-addled exterior, and finding my way back in through the window I'd used the last time. No. No chance. I was already dreading the return journey through the foul ether and the last thing I wanted was to subject myself to the thick soup I'd need to wade through. I just had to guess. You'd think, if this really was a trap, then the architect of this predicament might have left some clues. You'd think.

I took the right-hand door. Afterall it was close to the corridors I'd traversed before and I might find a familiar landmark to kickstart my sense of direction. It was doubtful; the place was massive, and I might just have to muddle through. I didn't relish the thought of walking into a trap and being blind-sided by a mysterious assailant, but there was little choice. I'd come here for answers; I wasn't leaving empty handed. No chance. I'd left the University with less than I'd started with and at least it was only my life on the line this time. That is, unless what Professor Lowe had told me was correct. A black hole. Not to be sniffed at. Maybe I wouldn't live to see this case to its end.

The hinges bawled out for oil after almost a decade of neglect and I thought to myself that I could very much do with some tender loving care myself. Maybe some oil too. And, by oil, I meant whiskey. The door groaned shut behind me and I found myself in a long corridor that was just as well-lit as everything else. I caught the grind and clank of the distant machinery; it was seeming less and less likely I was alone.

Offices lined the hallway, empty and dark through their glass doors; they were perhaps the only thing not touched by the recent radiance within the facility. I was on edge. My fingers stroked the handle of my gun in my jacket and I couldn't help but dart my eyes back and forth and peer into each room as I passed. I didn't want to be caught by surprise. Eight years ago, I'd felt the same way exploring this building, and despite finding myself in a different section, it all seemed too familiar. The only difference was the light.

There was another set of double doors ahead; where they led, I didn't know. Maybe the current occupier was only a security robot, maybe not. I had to keep going. I needed to find out. Whatever reason I'd left Space Station Delta to come here for was superseded by finding out why the lights were on, who was here. Or even what.

I pushed through the doors and was met with another corridor, shorter this time and without the series of offices. I must be getting close. An empty security desk stood at the other end next to yet another set of double doors. It had to lead to the main lab, the one where I had the accident. The grumble of the equipment was louder now, and it drowned any evidence of another occupant in the building. I withdrew my gun. I needed to be ready. This was all too familiar, trawling the corridors of strange facility, expecting to be accosted by a mysterious assailant at any moment. History repeating itself. I didn't relish spending another five years trapped in a time vortex.

This door was unlocked too.

I entered.

Yes. This is where it'd been. The vortex. The accident. I briefly wondered if the other doors in the reception would've led to the same place and whether I'd been caught in the ineffable bullshit web of destiny. Still, it was fortuitous I was here. Again. I could see the grated walkway above from all those years ago. I could hear the hum and grind of the computers and machinery around me. I could smell the electric fizzle.

It hadn't changed one bit. The two pillars, where I'd fallen, stood astride an empty space. Thankfully.

I moved a little further into the room.

Professor Lowe had told me that Subject B was planning on recreating the vortex. Was this why the facility was so alive? Was he here now? Would I finally find out his identity?

I fell sideways and hit the floor hard. Someone had barrelled into me. My breath was knocked from my chest and old injuries in my torso screamed at me. My head slammed against the tiled ground beneath me. Spots and stars filled my eyes. Dizzy. I tried to turn my head through the pain, tried to force my vision to clear. A thin figure stood over me. My gun, which was miraculously still in my hand, moved on instinct and aimed at the blurred someone who'd assaulted me. They kicked out and the weapon was torn from my grasp; I heard it clatter some distance away.

I was at a disadvantage.

I sucked at the air, filling my winded lungs. The figure towered over me; they had their own gun. I tried to focus but was still disorientated. Bones ached, my head pounded, and the straps of my respirator had twisted enough to dig into the skin of my neck.

I must be concussed, hallucinating. Or was I unconscious, trapped in a dream, a nightmare.

My attacker wasn't Subject B. It wasn't the masked man that had haunted me a few days ago.

It was a ghost.

A ghost.

It wasn't possible.

He was dead.

Dead.

His body... there'd been so much blood.

Lifeless.

I didn't understand.

Sam.

Sam was alive.

And he had a gun pointed at my head.

18. Surprise

"How…?"

Sam stood over me; he was angry, face reddened with rage.

"You're alive… Sam…" I said. "What…?"

"Quiet, Jack." It was the first time I'd heard his voice in days; it felt longer, almost a lifetime ago. A lot had happened since I found his body.

"How are you…?"

"I said, quiet," Sam repeated. "You need to stay quiet." He was shaking and I couldn't tell if it was anger or nerves. I'd never seen him fire a gun before, yet alone hold one; perhaps he was worried about accidently shooting me with it.

"You wouldn't, couldn't, hurt me," I said. I reached up to take the gun from my former lover. "Let me…"

"Shut up!" He knocked my hand away with the nozzle. "Shut up, shut up, shut up!" He cocked the hammer and took a step back. The gun's aim never left my head as he moved away. "Stand," he said.

I didn't move.

"I'm serious, Jack," said Sam. "Get up."

"No." I shook my head. "You're not going to fire on me. You'd never."

The long-haired man took a deep breath; he exhaled slowly. "You don't know me, not one bit."

"Yes, yes I do," I said. "You're Sam Whittle. You own a bar in Sector Six. You're kind and gentle. You love romantic music, even though I hate it. You love... me."

"Love you? Love you?!" Sam's face briefly transformed; he laughed. I'd never seen him like this. "Love you?? You don't even love yourself! Ha! How can I love someone with so much hate? So much vile, disgusting hate in their heart! You're a user, Jack. You use people; you put them through the wringer, spit them out and then push them to the very pits of despair! You don't know me. You don't know yourself; you have no idea who you really are."

"Sam..." I said. "I think you're being a little overdramatic."

"Overdramatic?" His face turned back to one of anger. "You shouldn't insult me; I'm holding the gun."

"Is this because I didn't want to take things further with you? I'm sorry, Sam, I really am." I shifted a little, propping myself up on my elbows. "They say you never miss something until it's gone. Sam. I thought you were dead." I tried to smile at him. "I've missed you; I really have."

"Is that why you ran straight to that damn whore after you found me dead?"

"I... I... I didn't know where else to go," I said. "I was upset. I needed someone who would understand. Someone to give me solace, comfort." There was more to it than simply comfort, but now wasn't the time for the truth. "Can't you understand that?"

"I'm no expert but I'm sure comfort isn't something you find in a vagina."

I opened my mouth in reply but was interrupted.

"Jack, I really don't care anymore. And, obviously, neither do you." His fingers tightened on the gun's grip and I could see his knuckles whiten. "The first chance you had you went running back to your past; you've never been able to move on after your accident. Never. You haven't changed one bit since you fell into that thing, the vortex. You can't commit to anything, especially people. You still sleep around with anything that moves, and I know you cheated on me while we were seeing each other."

"I wouldn't call it cheating," I said. "We, me and you, we were, our relationship was just a bit of fun. Nothing serious. I thought you knew that."

"I wanted more," said Sam. "I told you over and over, but you didn't listen. You just kept stringing me along, and whenever I tried to leave, you'd talk me into staying; you'd tell me of all the great things we'd do together, things we never did. You promised the world and gave me," he used one hand to gesture above and around him, "planet Earth. You gave me shit. I fell for it all, hook, line and sinker. You're a damn bastard, Jack."

"It was never my intention to hurt you, Sam. I loved you... I still love you."

"Bullshit."

"It's not too late," I said. "Sam, you're alive! I thought I'd never see you again! We can try again. Try and make it work. I admit, I should've treated you better and I'm sorry, but, Sam, we were good together, weren't we? I want to settle down with you. Move on, like you said. Come on, Sam, give me one more chance."

"It's too late," he replied. "And it's not enough."

"Why not?"

"You broke me, Jack." His eyes were wet, cheeks red. "You broke my heart and..." a tear rolled down his face, "I'm fixing that now. I'm fixing everything."

"Why?" I nodded toward the gun. "Why like this?"

"It's part of his plan," said Sam. He wiped his face with the back of his hand.

"Plan? Does it have something to do with the time vortex? Something to do with this place?"

"That would be telling."

"I know it has something to do with my accident, Sam," I said. "You said I haven't moved on from it, but, how can I? Everything seems to be leading me here. Even you."

"It's not all about you," he said. "You weren't the only one to fall into the vortex."

"I know. Subject B."

Sam didn't say anything.

"Tell me, who is Subject B? Is it Augustus Smith?"

"It really doesn't matter." Another tear trickled out from his green eyes. "You don't matter. To me, at least. I've moved on. And he's already left here; I only stayed behind to make sure you didn't interfere."

"I didn't think you were the type to date a killer, Sam. Especially a serial killer."

"What?"

"Augustus Smith. The Emerald Killer," I said. "He's who you're seeing now. The other person involved in my accident. Subject B."

"You think you know everything, Jack, but you really don't. He's not who you think he is."

"Then, who is he?"

Sam shrugged. "You'll see." He motioned with the gun for me to stand. "Get up. I need you to put you somewhere safe so I can leave without you following."

"You're not going to kill me?"

He raised his eyebrows.

"You won't hurt me," I said. "You'd never even hurt a fly."

A grin creeped up one side of my former lover's face. "Really? You really don't have any idea what I'm capable of." He laughed. It was disconcerting, the way he laughed. I didn't like it. "Tell me, Jack, how is Jill?"

"She's..." And then, it clicked in my brain. I really didn't know Sam at all, did I? I didn't think he could ever do anything like that. Never. He was always so compassionate and caring. I'd never seen him with a gun before today. No. That was a lie. He must have had a gun when I was with Jill in the University. He'd killed her. He'd shot Jill. He'd stolen her from me.

"She deserved it," said Sam. "You're better off without her; you can move on now." He gestured again for me to stand.

I complied, silently. My heart was pounding in my chest and my blood boiled. I'd never felt like this toward Sam before; I'd only wanted to love him in the past. Red mist filled my eyes. I'd never thought him capable of anything like this. He was right. I never knew who he was.

"Face the wall," said Sam.

I began to turn, cogs reeling in my brain, telling me to act.

Now, was my chance.

I spun on the spot and barrelled into my former lover. Sam grunted as I winded him, slammed into his chest, and pushed him backwards. My weary muscles objected to the sudden activity, but I had to stop him. I screamed. My hands seized the gun and I wrestled for control of the weapon. I tried to kick at the skinny man's legs, to trip and down him, but he managed to dodge and weave away from my attack. I needed to overpower him. We tussled. We pushed back and forth across the floor of the lab; he was looking into my eyes, a mixture of fear and anger in his expression. I was angry. He'd killed Jill. He'd killed her. I'd loved her. Loved him.

I pushed his arms down and shoved my full weight against him. He staggered back, collided with the wall. I felt his breath against me as it was expelled from his chest and the impact winded him. His head knocked against the wall. He struggled against me, but the smaller man was no match for me. He stopped fighting against me. I had him pinned.

"Jack…" he squeaked, his voice nothing more than a whisper.

I was tired and my lungs laboured; I didn't know what to say, what to do. I was enraged. But this was Sam. I couldn't…

Sam's face become a blur and excruciating pain roared throughout my being, a crescendo of agony that drained away my strength. I hadn't heard the gun go off, but I'd felt it. My legs gave way beneath me. I fell to the ground. My leg was warm, wet, and the feeling creeped across my skin; the fabric of my trousers was sodden, and a pool was forming beneath me. An agonising pressure gripped my thigh.

Sam had shot me. He'd goddamned shot me.

My former lover kneeled beside me. His hands flailed about, seemingly unsure what to do, and I could tell, even though the fuzziness, that he was crying.

"Jack," he said. "I'm… I'm sorry; I didn't mean to…"

"No." I kept my hand pressed against the wound; the blood wasn't slowing. "No, Sam… you meant it." It was hard to talk, hard to breathe.

"Jack, I…"

"Get away… from me." He'd killed Jill, shot her. I didn't want him anywhere near me; my heart hurt more than the gunshot wound and the closer he was, the more painful it seemed. "Go…"

"But, Jack…" I felt his hand on my shoulder. "I…"

"No, Sam." Everything seemed so distant. I was losing a lot of blood. "Go!"

The bartender stood but stayed near.

"Go!" I screamed at him with every ounce of strength I had left.

He took a few steps back. "I'm sorry, Jack, I really am." He took a final look at me and hurried away. I heard the door slam shut as he left me.

I was alone. I was alone, bleeding and hurt, with no-one to help me.

Consciousness drifted away.

19. Blood

I woke up, weak and still in pain. I didn't know how long I'd been unconscious, the lights in the facility still strained down from above and masked the passage of time in outside world.

I reached into my pocket for my SmartBoy; I needed help, needed to know how long I'd been here. It was smashed, broken into pieces from the scuffle with Sam.

Damn.

I was on my own.

At least my wedding ring was still there. Fat lot of good it would do me now.

This place, this facility, was where it had all gone downhill eight years ago and now, it seemed, it would be the place of my death.

Unless, I could find a med kit in this damn place. And even then, I wasn't out of the woods. I'd lost a lot of blood. It was almost as if I'd pissed myself; I lay in a pool of sticky and cloying redness that had soaked through my clothes and skin.

I looked around the lab. Above was the grated walkway I entered the lab through all those years ago. And across from me, the doors I'd entered through today. This place hadn't changed, however, the machines and equipment around me were silent now, and I was left with only the humming, buzzing lights. They machines had served their purpose, whatever that was.

If I was in charge of a laboratory, where would I keep the med kit?

It had to be close, right?

There was a desk near the far wall, just underneath the stairway coming down from the gangway above. That would make sense. Surely, they wouldn't put a med kit too near the machines. Not with the chemicals and drugs usually stored within.

I couldn't stand, not with the gunshot wound in my thigh, and I was still weak from the blood loss; I tried but instantly regretted it.

I turned onto my stomach and screamed as the bullet shifted; more blood seeped out and I wondered how much of it was actually left inside my veins rather than on my clothes and the floor. I must look a mess. A bloody mess. I certainly felt it. I was running on fumes and the effort of just a slight movement had exhausted me. I didn't know how I was going to make it from here to there, the little desk under the stairs, and it might be for naught; I didn't know for sure there was a med kit there.

I needed a drink.

It could dull the pain. And my senses, make things just a little easier.

If only I'd brought my hip flask with a little whiskey. Just to take the edge off.

I only had cigarettes in my jacket, but I was too dizzy to smoke them.

Damn it.

I just needed to push through. I could have all the alcohol and cigarettes I wanted once I was out of this situation. If I survived this.

I pulled myself along the floor, a trail of blood mapping my progress to my possible salvation. Each centimetre, every little millimetre, agony, a lifetime. The desk came no closer. It was getting harder and harder to move, and with each advance it drained more and more of my energy. My vision, still blurred and unfocused, drifted in and out of darkness.

But I pushed on.

And on.

For a moment, Sam was waiting, smiling with his arms crossed, waiting for me at the far end of the room. He was the help I needed. I called out his name, but it was just a shadow, a provocative hallucination sent from Hell to taunt me.

Damn it. Sam had shot me. Shot me!

I really needed to stop the bleeding.

I lay there for moment and gathered my strength.

I must've passed out again; I found myself coming to with no memory of going.

I returned to my plight and dragged myself a little closer to my destination. An inch was all I accomplished before I stopped again.

The murmur of the lights above me was comforting, a lullaby trying to send me to sleep, massaging my senses and trying to tempt me into the afterlife. A devil in disguise. I had to fight it. I had to get to the med kit.

I had to stop him. Subject B.

I pulled myself along.

He wasn't going to best me. He'd already turned Sam against me. And Jill was dead because of him. It was obviously personal, whatever his motivations, and it seemed he bore a grudge. I would too, if were him. I'd had a life after the time vortex.

And now, I was bleeding on the floor.

I was making progress; the desk was almost within reach. Through my blurred eyesight I could make out a white box on the wall, which was the worst place it could be. Out of reach from my prostrated body.

I thought back to what Professor Lowe had told me. Back in the elevator. Subject B was going to recreate the accident. Why? I had no idea. And as for who he was. Everyone was deliberately keeping me out of the loop.

I reached the desk. I was close, but not close enough. I still, somehow, needed to get the med kit from the wall.

I tried to stand again but I was still too weak; I'd left a path of smeared blood across the length of the lab, blood that should be within my body. My body cried out for it. Ached to be filled with blood once more. I was already sick of being in pain. Sick of everything. Staying alive was certainly becoming a chore.

I needed to find some way of getting to the med kit. I kicked at the table with my good leg, hoping to knock something useful from its surface. The desk shifted and its contents rattled. I kicked again, harder this time.

Electronic equipment, books and other detritus tumbled down. Kicking the damn thing was a double-edged sword. A metal cube, something sciency, slammed into my wounded thigh and I cried out with several loud and choice swears. It hurt. Blood, which I didn't think I had left inside me, leaked from the gunshot. Damn it. Still, some of this junk could be useful.

The metal cube, now with splatters of my inner workings, was close enough to reach without too much effort. I picked it up. If I could aim it just right, with enough force, I could knock the med kit from the wall. Hopefully.

I was in a lot of pain. The pressure on my leg was intense and I could no longer feel my toes at the other end; there were pins and needles along my limbs and torso, and my skin looked pale against the blood staining it. I felt like I was going to pass out again. I couldn't. I couldn't lose consciousness again; it might be last time I did.

I took a few deep breaths to gather my strength and tried to focus my eyes on the target. I might only have one shot.

I hurled the cube.

It smacked into the corner of the med kit, which rocked from the impact, and fell to the floor. The med kit was still on the wall.

Damn it.

I needed a damn drink.

I hooked my hands on the legs of the table and heaved; my body shifted, just a little, but it was enough for the metal cube to be within my reach once more. I was also closer to the med kit.

I threw the box once more.

This time, I was lucky. The med kit careened from the wall and landed on the other side of the desk. Not so lucky.

My salvation was almost at hand.

I just wanted to sleep, leave it all behind. My energy was draining away; it had drained away. I didn't have anything left. The med kit was so close, yet so far. I just needed one final push and everything I needed would be in that white box.

My wounded leg didn't feel part of me anymore; it had been emptied of its blood, replaced with pain. The prickling sensation was everywhere now, even in my head and in my eyes. Everything seemed so distant. Fizzy. The room was getting dark; someone had hit the dimmer switch.

I felt sick. Hungry. My head was spinning.

I forced myself to shuffle along the floor and, with outstretched arm, caught the edge of the med kit with my fingertips. My skin, wet with my own blood, slipped along the plastic and the box only moved a fraction. I fought. I pressed down and pulled. The box rocked and edged toward me. Almost. Almost there. I tried to move my own body a little closer and, as I shifted, the tingle under my skin felt like a cheese grater against the floor.

At last.

I caught hold of the box and brought it near to my chest.

It popped open.

Ah! Beautiful drugs!

And bandages, of course, both the fabric and liquid kind.

But the drugs were the more important thing. At least they would ease the pain and do something for the blood loss. I mean, they were probably, almost definitely out of date, but at this point, anything would do.

I grabbed one of the injector pods and tried to make out the medicinal name through my fuzzy vision. 'T...' something. That was probably a pain killer. I tucked it next to me. I needed something to give me a kick first. I grabbed another. This one was 'Z...' something something '...mine.' That would be it. I jammed the end of the injector into my arm. I felt an instant rush. The pins and needles intensified into a full-on ache along my whole body and my heart pounded fast and hard. Fresh blood trickled from the wound on my thigh. That was definitely the right stuff.

The room brightened and my vision cleared; I was still dizzy, but the stimulant had done its job. I was awake. Fully awake. I just needed to deal with the gunshot problem before the false and fleeting feeling of alertness killed me. My pulse raced; the blood loss had increased.

I rummaged through the white box for a liquid bandage. There would be no point removing the bullet; I wasn't a surgeon, and I was guaranteed to make it worse. In my time as a police officer I'd seen bullet removals go south fast; the bullet was usually the only thing keeping the rest of the victims' blood inside their body. I would be no different, and I was very lucky Sam hadn't hit an artery or I'd already be dead.

The liquid bandage spray was two years out of date. Still, the coagulant within should stem the bleeding at least for now, and the local anaesthetic in the foam should ease the pain. The bandage would only be a temporary fix. I needed a hospital and I was at least four hundred kilometres from the nearest. Earth, famously, no longer had even one.

I ripped at the hole in my trousers, widening my access to the injury. There was a hole. A red pond overflowing, oozing and dribbling along my skin. I dabbed it with some absorbent pads and cleared away some of the excess blood.

I took a deep breath.

Quick was probably better, right?

I jammed the nozzle of the liquid bandage into the opening and squeezed the trigger. I screamed to the empty room, clenched and gritted my teeth; the sting of the foam was even more painful than the wound itself.

The cannister clattered to the floor and I took a few moments to gather myself. A whole new level of hurt was coursing through me, pulsing and spreading its tendrils throughout my body. There were spots in my eyes. I couldn't breathe. I couldn't bring myself to take a breath. I just needed the pain to pass and then I could continue tending to my injury. It would pass. It had to. I closed my eyes; the spots remained and flashed with every throb. My head spun.

I forced myself to take in some air. It was easing, either that or I was accustomed to it, but it was enough to allow me to take another look at my leg. The hole was gone. Damned by the bandage. There was a bubbly and pink deformed mass affixed to my leg; the bandage had spilled over from its organic receptacle and caused me to grow a malformed tumour of foam. I touched it gingerly with my fingertips; it was already starting to solidify. I quickly evened the surface with some pads and cleansed the area around it.

I needed another boost; I was lagging a little. I took another dose of the stimulant and felt its instant rush yet again.

It occurred to me, all alone in this lab, in this facility on Earth, there was no-one else here. The lights might be on, but only for me. I looked over to the two metal towers. No vortex had spawned between them. Not here. Subject B was going to recreate the accident, but it was going to happen somewhere else.

I rummaged through the med kit and dug out some more absorbent pads. There wasn't many left in there; I'd used most of them sopping up the blood around the bullet hole. I stuck some of the remaining ones onto my skin. I needed to pad out the liquid bandage with the real thing; out of date medical supplies would be unreliable and I didn't want my leg to resume leaking.

Subject B was going to recreate the accident in Howard's lab at the University.

If I was going to get out of here alive, that was where I needed to be.

I tore some fabric from the inside of my jacket, a strip, and tied it tight around my leg. Not only would it help to hold the pads over the wound, it would act as another failsafe, a tourniquet.

I pulled out the painkiller injector, the 'T...' something, and stabbed it into my leg.

It counteracted the stimulant immediately; I felt a wave of ease drift over me and I felt myself dropping off. A dreamless sleep. Relaxed.

I slept, I didn't know how long for, but whatever was in that last injector had helped; I was still in pain, but it was distant. My leg felt stiff, but I could walk on it, at least, with a little help from a broom as a crutch. I filled my pockets with the remaining supplies from the med kit. The stimulant was the most important right now; I had no SmartBoy, it was still busted up from the fight, and no way of contacting an autocar.

It was going to be an arduous trek to the transport station.

I indulged in a cigarette.

A long arduous trek with that damn respirator.

20. Home

Without my SmartBoy I had no way of tracking the time, but by my estimate is that it took over three hours to get from the facility to the transport station and if it wasn't for liberal use of the stimulant from the med kit, I'd have never made it. The drugs were all definitely out of date; it wasn't my first rodeo, using field medicine, and the medical supplies certainly didn't have the results they were supposed to have. The liquid bandage hadn't numbed the pain quite as it should and didn't fully solidify; I felt the gooey foam dribbling out from under the pads and down my leg a couple of times during my long trek. It was disgusting. The painkiller injector made me fill dizzy; it probably wasn't meant to be used alongside the stimulant, but I chalked its side effects up to its expiry. And I'd managed to ignore the hallucinations.

But I made it. I'd only thrown up eight times.

It was getting dark outside, marginally so; the thick pollution outside didn't usually discriminate between that of the sun's illumination and that of the chemical streetlights.

The slight difference in lighting was the only marking of time, aside from the clock on the wall of the transport station.

I'd been on Earth and away from home for three days; most of which I must've been unconscious. It felt like longer.

I threw off the uncomfortable respirator as soon as I entered the empty station; I didn't know what was worse, the tight breathing apparatus or the gunshot wound. Both were painful and laborious to endure. I handed the mask at the desk and, after checking my identity mugshot on her screen, collected a duplicate return ticket from a rather gruff looking woman; she kept looking me up and down with a confused expression. She was probably wondering what I was doing there, covered in dried blood and resting on a broom. I asked her where I could get cleaned up and she pointed me to the restroom.

The facilities were reflective of my current state, minus the blood; although there was a little already in one of the sinks. The joys of public toilets. Dirt and grime covered the floors and walls, amongst other things, and looking in the mirror, I looked like I fit right in with the décor. I'd managed to get blood everywhere; not only was it covering my damaged leg, but it was smeared along the side of my body. My hands were caked in dried blood. I'd even managed to get some on my face. The browned, rusty and scaly blood had blended with the yellow dust of the outside environs, and the only exception was where the straps of my respirator had cut into the skin of my face; red marks denoted their previous location. My clothes were tattered and ruined, filthy. I did my best to clean up with the cheap soap and even cheaper toilet paper; I made myself somewhat respectable. A respectable tramp. I still looked a mess.

I dug out some of the medical supplies from my pockets. The makeshift tourniquet on my leg, as well as the absorbent pads were bloodied and soiled; I needed to change them. I topped up the liquid bandage and redressed the wound; my jacket suffered again, and I bound the fabric tighter around my leg than the last one. I used the last of the stimulant and tossed the empty injector into the overflowing bin.

I hobbled out into the waiting room and sat down. The departure boards were an unwelcome sight; the next elevator to Space Station Delta wasn't until the morning. I was going to be stuck here all night. At least I wasn't alone. The place was quiet, but I wasn't the only person here; aside from the grumpy clerk at the ticket desk, there were also one or two bums buzzed off their faces on the most recent drug craze and passed out on the seating across from me, an old lady knitting in the corner and a multitude of local fauna scurrying along the edges of the room. Perfect company for the evening.

I caught sight of a vending machine and limped over to it; my stomach rumbled at the sight and I realised I hadn't eaten since leaving the space station. I might have to make do with window shopping; I'd almost forgotten about my broken SmartBoy. I glanced around. The other travellers were too wrapped up in their own business to pay attention to me and the receptionist was almost asleep. I'd have to employ something an old friend had shown me. It wasn't strictly legal. In fact, it was entirely illegal. But needs must. And it would only work on older vending machines which this one, fortunately was. I jimmied open the selection screen and exposed the wires within. I squeezed and held two of the wires together with my fingertips. This was gonna sting. I tapped something, anything, on the screen. Electric zapped, there was a small crackle and some smoke. I hastily closed up the opening and sucked on my fingers; the pain was nothing compared to what I'd been through over the last couple of days.

Now, to see if my efforts had worked.

I selected a cake bar and crossed my fingers.

The machine creaked and beeped.

And dumped all its contents in the collecting tray at the bottom.

I checked my audience; it was only the lady behind the desk. She was awake and staring. I shrugged at her in response and she went back to her nap. She didn't seem that concerned, and I guessed this wasn't the first time someone had busted the vending machine. That was good for me; I didn't need any security or police sniffing around. I was starving. I knelt by the opening and took only what I needed; I left the rest for the lucky fucker who followed me.

I returned to my seat, filled up on junk, and dozed until the automated voice announced boarding for the elevator. It was the first one of the next day; the only passengers were me, the knitting lady and a small number of commuters.

The transport set off and I distracted myself by listening to the inane conversations around me. It was a welcome diversion from my own dramas; apparently someone had been murdered in Sector Six. The body had been left disfigured and mauled. Gruesome. But murder wasn't unusual. Not for Sector Six. My home sector was almost as despicable as Sector Seven and it was often that the worst of society found themselves there. Murderers, thieves, rapists; they kept me in business when there were no philandering spouses or missing cats to pursue. I tuned out the discussion. I just needed to rest. Well, I needed to go to the hospital, but I had more important things to deal with.

Subject B.

I hoped I wasn't too late. There was no telling how soon it would be before he tried to create the time vortex, recreate the experiment. Lives were at stake. Mine could wait.

I considered going to Suede and Johnson and telling them what was going on, but it was too unbelievable. They already didn't trust me; they would likely lock me up again and tell me I was a danger to myself and others. Especially in the state I was in now. Telling them that billions were going to die was probably above their pay grade; it wasn't exactly parking tickets.

The other option was Dionne Bex. Surely, she'd want to know what twisted scheme had erupted from a former employee's actions. I mean, she knew about the experiments on Subject B; it was all in the files she'd handed over. But what could she do? She was paying me to deal with it; she didn't want Tribeca Systems involved. Publicly, at least. Ms Bex wanted plausible deniability and if I went to her that would be out the window. Tribeca Systems did not involve itself in world ending bullshit. She'd certainly be reluctant to pay me if I asked for her help.

I only had one option. I had to go there myself. Go to the University and stop Subject B. And Sam.

My leg twinged. I was out of painkillers.

I'd lost my gun in the facility; I couldn't go there unarmed. I'd need to get to my office first, pick up my spare firearm and head straight over to Sector Three.

And it would have to be on foot.

Well, foot and broom. My improvised crutch was the only companion I had left, and I was without my SmartBoy; I couldn't order an autocar to shuttle me around the space station. And big corporations like Tribeca Corp wouldn't exactly give free rides to people trying to stop the end of the world.

The elevator reached Space Station Delta and all passengers alighted, including me.

I lit up a cigarette as soon as I left the transport hub. I was almost out and made a mental note to pick up some more from my desk drawer.

A quick drink would be most welcome too.

I hobbled along through the morning streets and made my way into Sector Six. It was quiet, still too early for most of the population and I found myself lighting up another cigarette. My leg still hurt, and the painkillers were beginning to wear off. The stiffness, however, had eased; I was able to abandon the broom and walk somewhat normally, yet painfully, unassisted.

The expired liquid bandage must be doing some good to allow me to walk.

I turned a corner.

My office was in view; I was almost home.

Damn.

Home was not somewhere I could go.

Outside the apartment building where I lived, where I worked, police and their vehicles gathered behind black and yellow barriers.

Damn it.

the final case of Jack Gemini

21. Frame

I backtracked, heading away from my office and back the way I came. Something was going down. Undoubtedly something to do with Subject B and I didn't have time for it. Not another distraction.

Once I was far enough away, I jumped into a SmartBoy terminal booth on one of the side streets. My own SmartBoy was useless in its current state, broken and inoperative, and I needed to rely on the public version for information on what was happening; it was something big. Multiple police units and the area cordoned off usually meant someone was dead. Murder, probably.

I broke open the wiring box and fiddled with some of the exposed circuits. It stank in here. Especially this low down. Stale urine. I'd forgotten these terminals often doubled as public bathrooms and I tried to ignore the fumes of ammonia which were trying their hardest to get me high. The screen flickered to life. It was somewhat cruel and senseless that you needed your SmartBoy to pay for things like this; a personal SmartBoy to pay for a public one. Fortunately for me I could bypass that.

I searched the local news and was greeted with a picture of my face. I wasn't surprised; I just wished they'd picked a more flattering picture. I certainly looked like a criminal. I was the prime suspect in a murder enquiry which certainly explained the strong police presence in Sector Six and, in particular, outside my apartment building. Framed. The victim was stripped naked and cut open, their insides spilled everywhere. The police and the press had good reason to suspect me. Especially considering the identity of the desiccated corpse; my involvement would be obvious and there was a decent case for my motivations.

It was Professor Howard Lowe.

My ex-wife's new husband and subject of my current case.

I was suspect number one.

There was even a reward for finding me.

Ha.

Ha ha.

I was out of credits and looked like a tramp.

Perhaps I could hand myself in and claim the reward? At least I'd be able to replace my SmartBoy. And my gun.

It was time to move.

Subject B held all the cards and he wasn't making things easy for me. Framed for a murder? Another one? Maybe I'd find out that Howard Lowe had faked his death too; my other leg could do with a bullet in it. To match the other one.

I needed to change my plans and head straight to the University. Unarmed. And without getting caught. Sector Three was two sectors away from me on the other side of Sector Eight. It usually annoyed me how the sectors had been arranged, out of order without rhyme or reason, but today, it was to my good fortune. Six, Seven, Eight. And then, Three. I was close to Seven's entrance now, and I could easily find a discrete way to Three from there.

I kept to the back alleys and side streets; the main problem would be large safety door that led inside. I hoped the cops weren't keeping watch. It was early and there wouldn't be many people around meaning my travel would easily be seen.

Thankfully, I was lucky, and the gateway was clear of the law.

I slipped through and ducked into an alley.

Subject B was making my life goddamned difficult.

I retrieved a cigarette from my jacket pocket; I only had three left. I lit up. No gun and hardly any smokes left. Subject B was going to pay for this.

"Ah, Mr Gemini," called a voice from behind, "we've been looking for you."

I turned to see the other pricks in my side, Detectives Suede and Johnson.

"You're Space Station Delta's most wanted," said Johnson. "Who'd have known you'd try and flee, eh?"

"I don't know what you're talking about," I said.

"Come off it," said Suede. "You wouldn't be skulking though Sector Seven if you weren't guilty of something."

"Oh, right; you're talking about Professor Lowe." I carefully placed my free hand in my pocket. I took a long drag of my cigarette. "I don't suppose you'd believe me if I told you it wasn't me." My fingers closed around the liquid bandage pod.

Suede laughed. Johnson too. They took a couple of steps toward me.

"I don't think you should come any closer," I said. I pushed the injector pod forward in my pocket. "I've got a gun."

"Really?" said the male cop. "I don't believe you."

"Can you really take the chance?" I moved back from them. "You saw what happened to Professor Lowe; do you want the same to happen to you?"

The two cops shared a glance.

"Stay where you are." I made a point of forcing the pod as forward as I could. Its nozzle poked against the fabric of my jacket. "I just want to talk, that's all."

Detective Suede crossed his arms. "Go on." He looked a little fed up. He nudged Johnson. "Let's hear what this dumbass has to say. Are you going to tell us you're innocent? That it's all a mistake. We've heard it all before, Mr Gemini."

"I am innocent," I said. "Of this, at least."

Suede raised his eyebrows. "Back-up's on its way. We called it in as soon as we saw you," he said. "Was that all you really wanted to talk about?"

"I didn't do it. I saw the professor at the transport hub recently; why would I kill him?"

"Oh, I don't know, I mean, it looks like he put up a fight." He gestured up and down. "You look a right mess."

"It's my own," I said. "It's a long story."

"You wanted to talk," said Johnson, chiming in. "Was it revenge for stealing your wife? Did Professor Lowe attack you first? And you killed him in self-defence? Although, I've got to admit, self-defence is a poor plea given the state you left him in."

"Jill hired me to find him."

"And you found him alright," said the woman. "You found his internal organs too, all over the floor."

"Johnson," warned Suede. "What have I told you about making quips?"

"Sorry, sir."

"The case is bigger than Howard Lowe," I said. "I was on my way to Earth when he told me..."

"And that's where you killed him," said Detective Suede. "There's video surveillance of you dragging his body through a checkpoint at the transport hub. That was last night. And before you say, 'that wasn't me,' you face is as clear as day; it was you. Not to mention, your DNA is plastered all over the body. And its entrails."

"Last night, you said?" I flicked the stub of cigarette to the floor.

The cop nodded.

"It can't have been me; this must all be an elaborate hoax." I tightened my grip on the bandage pod. I needed to get out of here. Before their back-up arrived. "I wasn't even on Space Station Delta at that time. I was on Earth. You can check."

"We will," said Suede. "Once you're safely locked up."

"And what about this?" I used my free hand to indicate my injured leg. "It's fresh, can't you see? Did the person dragging Lowe through the checkpoint have a gunshot wound?"

"Sloppy work. You need a new doctor."

"Well, was the suspect injured? You call yourself cops."

"No, but..."

"I dragged myself halfway across the planet with a damn bullet in my leg," I said. "I got to the station this morning. I didn't kill Professor Lowe."

"You can say what you like," said Johnson. "It doesn't change anything; you're still wanted for murder. Again. You seem to get mixed up in this sort of thing far too often for my liking."

"And I was innocent the other times, was I not?"

Detective Johnson shrugged. "You're certainly clever enough to get away with it; you were a cop after all. A dirty one."

"You give me too much credit." I sighed. "But I know who did it."

"You?"

"Go on," said Suede. "Tell us."

"I don't have a name," I said. I had a plan of escape; I gripped the cannister in my pocket. "He's known as Subject B."

"I bet you can't even give us a description."

"No, but I have to stop him. He's dangerous. Subject B is going to create a time vortex that will suck in everything around it; he's going to kill billions of people."

Suede laughed. "That's the most bullshit thing I've ever heard, Mr Gemini. Next, you'll be telling us that this Subject B fellow is an alien. It's absurd. How in Hell could we believe something like that?"

"It doesn't really matter," I said. "I'm leaving soon, whether you like it or not."

"Right..."

"I'll even tell you where I'm going; you can catch me up. And bring your back-up along." I psyched myself up for my escape plan. "I'm heading to the University to stop Subject B."

"You really believe that bullshit, huh?"

I nodded.

"Why are you telling us your plan?" said Johnson. "Why the University?"

"I just want a head start," I said. I was ready to go. "That's where he's going to do it. Subject B."

"Don't be stupid." Suede uncrossed his arms and took a step forward. "You need to come with us."

I retreated a little. "By the way, detectives," I said. I didn't want this going off too close. "I haven't got a gun." I hurled the liquid bandage at the floor. The cannister exploded, white gas and liquid spurted everywhere, and the cops covered their eyes in defence. I was briefly invisible. In the confusion I jumped forward and disarmed Suede. I had a gun, his gun. I aimed it at my two pursuers. They both put their hands up.

"Cuff her," I said to Detective Suede. "Cuff yourself to her."

"Now, wait a minute," said the cop, "you don't think you're going to get away with this, do you?"

"I said, cuffs! Cuff yourself to each other." I waved the gun about to show I meant business. "Now!" I wasn't going to shoot; I just needed them to believe that I would.

"Back-up's on the way," said Johnson as Suede reluctant handcuffed her. "You're being stupid."

"I know." I took a few steps back and watched as the two police detectives were linked together. "Call it in. Tell your bosses what I'm doing."

Detective Suede started to step forward.

I fired the gun.

The pair ducked instinctively. They had nothing to worry about; I shot at the wall. But it did give me another distraction.

I ran. I pushed through the pain in my leg and ran as fast as I could.

Subject B be might be starting the vortex.

He might've already begun.

22. Mirror

There was no sign of pursuit from the inept detectives. Or anyone else for that matter. I didn't know whether they'd heeded my advice and called for back-up. Probably. I was a wanted criminal after all, and it would look good for them to catch someone who'd done something so gruesome. Then again, they didn't want to look stupid. They had me. And I outwitted them. It hadn't been difficult; they were the type of cops to take things for granted. They saw everything in black and white. Good guys and bad guys. They wanted to be heroes. Ha. They needed a dose of the real world.

I found my way into the autocar underpass. A little dangerous, but I just needed to find the service door; I could easily slip into Sector Three and the University if I travelled the maintenance tunnels. Maintenance. That was a joke. They were never used for maintenance, only repairs as and when they happened and were needed. It was one of the benefits of living in such a frugal society; they, the bigwigs, were always thinking of the cost and, of course, it was expensive to maintain the underpass. But it was to my advantage; the tunnels would be empty, and I could slip between sectors without the worry of being caught. The downside was having to sidestep along the wall, especially with my wounded leg; it was difficult, and I needed to be careful not to slip from the narrow curb and into traffic. Granted, it wasn't busy at this time in the morning, but I knew, from a past case that autocars stop for no-one. I didn't fancy being smeared along the highway.

I reached a depressed section of the wall and slipped in and away from the roads. My leg ached and stung; the anaesthetic in the liquid bandage was wearing off, so were the drugs, and I was certain the wound was bleeding again. It would have to wait; there was no time. I bust open the lock of the service door with a well-aimed strike from the handle of the gun I'd stolen from the dopey detectives and entered the tunnel.

I felt like I was pushing myself to my limits, rushing along the dark corridors; I hadn't recovered from exertions on the planet, nevermind my exertions running away from Suede and Johnson. I needed to rest. I needed to get this damned bullet out from my thigh.

I needed to stop that damned lunatic.

It was dark, dingy, and I wished my SmartBoy wasn't so bust up; I could've done with the extra light just to clearly see the maps found on every junction. The dim yellow lighting was insufficient. I was certain they'd be a hatch that opened straight up into the University's grounds; I just needed to get there. And quickly. Without getting lost.

I squinted at the latest. I was close.

The distant sounds of autocars racing along the underway was picking up and the chug of the wheels along the roadways became more frequent; the day was moving along too fast and rush hour was starting. Oh, how little they knew. Above their heads their little worlds could end at any moment.

So, could mine.

I turned a corner. I tripped, my leg buckled, and my face smashed into the wall. I crumpled to the floor. Damn. Damn it. My head rung, vision spinning, and I felt fresh blood trickle down my face, my leg too. Everywhere hurt. Again. The bullet wound cried out for even more attention than it'd already had. I was sick of it, sick of being in goddamned pain.

I pulled myself up to a sitting position and lit up one of the last few cigarettes in my possession. It was difficult to get cigarettes in prison these days. Alcohol was even rarer. If only I'd kept a hip flask in my jacket. For emergencies. I made a mental note to always carry one at all times in the future. If there was one.

I sucked up some smoke. I needed to savour the taste; it might be a long time before I could enjoy a cigarette again.

I touched my head and my fingertips came back red; I'd cut my temple on the wall. It was minor and would easily heal. I was pretty certain I didn't have concussion but, if I did, there was nothing I could do about it; I was very much at the whims of fate and I didn't have time to muck about. Except for this cigarette, of course.

My leg, on the other hand, was a little more serious; there was blood seeping out from underneath the absorbent pad I'd tied to my thigh. My hodgepodge first aid had lasted longer than I thought especially considering everything I'd used was past its prime. I undid my makeshift tourniquet and lifted the pad below. Ergh. An angry hole stared back at me. It did not look pleased at my choice of abandoning the remaining liquid bandage in my daring escape; it could certainly use a bit more. A top up.

I stubbed out the cigarette and pulled a fresh spongey pad from my pocket. I'd have to make do. I couldn't get to a hospital. Not yet. Not with the cops on my tail and a madman to catch. I applied the pad and tied the remnants of my suit back around my thigh, gritting my teeth as I pulled it tight, tighter than it'd been before. I needed to make sure I didn't bleed to death in these tunnels or my body would never be found.

I clambered to my feet. My leg felt weak and it hurt but I pushed through the pain. I hobbled on through the service tunnels to my destination.

Fortunately, for me and my haggard body, it didn't take long to find the section below Solaris University. I squinted at the map. Yes. I was right. There were several access points across the whole campus. I just needed to find the right one. I traced my finger along the lines and shapes; I just needed to find whichever was closest to Howard's lab and I was in.

I carried on walking through the buttery corridors but with a destination mapped out.

I didn't really have much of a plan.

Scratch that.

I didn't have a plan at all.

All I had was my wits and my gun. And my wits were at the end of their tether.

And it wasn't my gun either; I'd stolen it from Suede.

I found what I was looking for. A ladder. And If I'd read the maps correctly, then this would come out somewhere near the lab.

I climbed. My wounded leg ached and throbbed with every rung; I winced every time I put pressure on it. There was a manhole at the top. With an electronic lock. For once, it would be nice if something worked out the way I wanted it to. It was never easy. I considered shooting the lock but decided against wasting a bullet. For the second time in the last hour, I used the handle as a hammer. The circuit box fell open and its plastic cover plummeted to the depths below me. Depths. It was only twice my height. I heard it clatter against the metal floor of the service tunnel.

I hooked my arm under one of the ladder rungs and with my free hand pulled on the wires. They sparked and fizzed. I covered my eyes from the burning embers that fired out at my face because the last thing I needed was to be blinded. I didn't really know what I was doing. I tried the manhole above. Just in case pulling the power had done anything. Nope. I fiddled with the wires. More sparks. It was difficult to do with one hand, but I managed to wire the power supply directly to the lock mechanism.

There were several clicks as the lock was overloaded. Then a clunk.

I was in.

I pushed up and slid the cover out of the way.

It was dark wherever I'd come out, whatever room in the University I entered. A basement of some sort? The meagre light from the tunnels below was barely registering in my eyesight and I thought for a moment I'd somehow got the electrical sparks in my eyes and blinded myself. Fortunately, there was sliver of light just ahead; light peeking out from under a door. It still wasn't enough to see where I was or to find my way around. But it was there. It smelled damp in here. Musty. And quiet. My ears only caught the distant drip of water on metal somewhere in the room.

I shuffled forward, with my hands conducting the darkness for any obstructions in my path. My leg couldn't take another fall, or a knock from another obstacle; it was still painful, still bleeding. I just needed to get to the light switch unharmed. I felt some sort of shelving unit to my right. I fingered the edges of the shelves until I was safely passed it. I reached the doorway. It was a little easier to see, this close to the light source, and I found the switch with ease.

The room illuminated.

I was in some sort of janitorial room; there were tools and cleaning equipment stacked along the shelving units, a sink in the corner and a multitude of brooms.

A first aid kit would be handy.

Surely, janitors got hurt sometimes.

I found one near the sink, where the dripping sound had originated, and quickly redressed the bullet wound. Fresh liquid bandage on top of the expired original wasn't ideal but it would do for now, and at least it would stop me leaking all over the University campus. I also topped up my blood stream with some stimulants and painkillers; pretty soon the wound on my thigh would be leaking more chemicals than blood.

There was a mirror in the little room; I looked a right state. There was no point trying to tidy myself up, no point even trying to look like I belonged on the campus. I just needed to get to the lab as soon as possible.

I crept to the door and peeked out into the corridor.

There was no-one about despite the time of day. It was familiar; I'd been here before. It was the corridor leading to the lab. How lucky for me that my orientation skills had worked on the unclear and confusing maps underground. I could hear voices to my right at the far end of the hall. The demonic purple haired receptionist was that way; thank fuck I was heading in the opposite direction.

I checked my pockets; the ring was still in my possession. It was too important. It was all I had left of Jill.

I slipped out of the closet and made my way to Howard's lab. This corridor, it made think of her. There was no evidence left of her, here in the University, aside from my memories; the police clean up after her death had made her disappear. The last time Jill and I had walked these halls she'd told me she'd slept with me because of nostalgia. It was bullshit. We'd slept together because of love. She'd denied it, told me we used each other to soothe our hearts, but I knew better. Jill had rejected my claims over and over, even as we still searched for clues about her missing husband inside the lab. She'd moved close to me, she'd kissed me... and...

I needed to focus; my own life was on the line now.

I pulled the gun from my jacket pocket, just in case, and held it low; anyone could enter this hallway at any time, and I didn't want to get caught armed by campus security. My hand fell on the handle of the door. There were distant voices inside, too distant to make out the words. I took one final look around and opened the door, only slightly. I slipped inside.

The office beyond was empty and dark. Light shone in through the big windows from the illuminated facility beyond. The source of the voices. I slunk a little further in, staying low, and peeped into the main lab. There were two men standing on a raised platform in front of one of the machines. One figure I knew very well; I could recognise his slender figure and long black hair anywhere, even from behind. It was Sam. He was arguing with the other man, something about where a particular dial needed to be set. The other man must be Subject B. The voice was familiar. So was his frame. But his identity was still a mystery to me.

I crept toward the double doors at the far side of the room. I needed to stay quiet, catch the pair by surprise. I pushed through into the lab and onto the steps leading down. I kept close to the wall, out of view. I could still hear them arguing; Subject B was telling Sam how he knew better, how he had experience of this sort of thing. Sam was telling him it didn't matter; he'd read the instructions. Goddamned fools were going to blow up everything because they couldn't agree.

I reached the bottom of the steps and, keeping my eyes on the two men's' backs, skulked closer. A white blob caught my peripherals; to my left, a white mask, sat on a table. The masked man. Subject B. There was no need for the disguise anymore. Not when he was this close to recreating the experiment.

Sam and Subject B were in front of a machine near the two pillars where the time vortex would be. I moved closer. I raised the gun.

This was it.

This was the moment I stopped him.

Sam's head turned, ever so slightly. I caught his eye and his mouth dropped. He spun. Looked right at me. Subject B was still talking.

"Jack," he said. He placed his hand on the other man's shoulder. "Jack."

"What?"

Subject B turned.

And I found out why Professor Lowe didn't want me to know who he was.

It was me.

I was Subject B.

the final case of Jack Gemini

23. Subject

It was like staring into a mirror, if that mirror had looked after himself better. Unlike me, the other Jack was clean shaven, tidy and well-dressed. It wasn't possible. How? How was there another me? It didn't make any sense. Plastic surgery? Look-alike? Long lost twin? What the goddamned fuck was going on?

Subject B... the unmasked man... he was staring at me.

I stared back.

I couldn't move. I couldn't believe what I was seeing.

I didn't notice Sam creeping close. A boot slammed into my injured thigh. I screamed. I fell to the floor, pain coursing through my leg and searing my whole being. Spots flashed before my eyes and I struggled to focus on anything but the hurt. I screamed again.

"I'm sorry," said the bartender. I felt his presence above me. He kicked me again. This time it was in the stomach. I barely felt it; the agony from my tortured leg felt like a leaden aura around me that dominated my other senses and feelings.

I was lifted up, dragged by my arms and placed in a chair. I couldn't fight back; my body just wanted to curl up into a ball and die. The pain throbbed. Everywhere. My limbs wouldn't respond to my commands and I felt like a marionette being pulled along by strings. Strings, rope, that tied my arms behind my back and my ankles to the legs of the chair. I tried to kick out, kick back at my captors, but nothing responded. I struggled to keep conscious. My surroundings started to fade as the pain started to take over everything.

"Wake up." My own voice was talking to me. "Wake up! Sam, give him the Zytreximine, will you? I need him awake."

Life flooded back to me; the stimulant did its thing and I watched as two figures become clear before me. One was Sam. The other...

"Glad you could join us," said Subject B. He grinned. "You can witness me take everything back." He held up his hand. It glinted. "This is mine." It was my wedding ring; he'd taken it from my pocket. "I had it once before, but you stole it a second time. My ring." He shoved it in his pocket and turned to Sam. "Keep an eye on him; if he's anything like me, he'll try something stupid." The 'other me' looked me up and down and walked back to the machine he was working on. "It's almost time." He opened a panel and pulled on some wires.

"I don't understand," I said. "Who are you?"

He stopped what he was doing and faced me. "I'm you." He giggled. "Or rather, you're me." He continued with his work on the wiring. "This will all be over soon, don't worry," he said. "Things will go back to normal."

"Normal? Normal?! You're going to blow everything up with that damned thing! You just told me: 'This will all be over soon, don't worry.' Everything will be over!"

Subject B ignored me and carried on with his work. I turned to Sam. He was pointing my own gun at me, well, the gun I'd acquired, at me.

"Sam," I said, "tell me what's going on? Just who is this guy?"

"He's you," said the bartender. He sighed. "Look, Jack, I'm sorry. I'm sorry about everything. I'm sorry that it had to come to this."

"I don't want any apologies from you; I don't want anything from you anymore."

"I'm sorry to hear that."

"More apologies? I told you I didn't want to hear it."

"It's all I've got, Jack. It's all I can offer you."

"You can offer me the truth," I said. The rope around my ankles and wrists was too tight; my leg was bleeding again, and I could feel the blood wettening my trousers. "Tell me who he is."

"I've already told you that; he's you."

"That doesn't make any sense. How could he be... me?"

"You stole his life, Jack." He pointed at me with his unarmed hand. "You were supposed to be the one experimented on, not him." He jabbed at the air in front of me. "You were the one who was supposed to suffer." He placed his hand on his heart and looked over to Subject B. "He and I were meant to be together, not you and me. Fate screwed him over."

"I've... suffered."

"Bullshit, Jack," said Sam. "You messed up his life."

"But how? I don't understand," I said. "This is my life, not his. He might look like me..."

"He doesn't just look like you, he is you."

"You keep saying that, but it doesn't make any sense!"

Subject B sighed and replaced the panel on the machine. He turned to me. "Do you know what Professor Lowe was working on?"

I shrugged, a difficult feat when bound to a chair.

"Take a guess, go on," he said. "You must've looked through the documents Ms Bex gave you."

"I don't know. I know it wasn't really a time vortex." I racked my brains. "It was something to do with parallel capacitational conduits. Something sciency."

"He was studying..." Subject B paused, eyes up as if reading from his memory. "Trans-capacitational Conduits and Parallel Sub-dimensional Acquisition Nodes. Something sciency, indeed. I don't really understand it myself, but there's one thing that's key to this whole thing."

"And that is?" He was toying with me.

"Parallel."

"What?"

Subject B, the other Jack, laughed. "Parallel. As in, parallel world, parallel you."

"You're from a parallel world?"

"No, Jack. You are," he said. "You're the one from another world."

"That can't be... right." Things hadn't added up since I started working on this case. "No, it can't be."

"Oh, it is. It's completely right. This is my world. My life."

"No..."

"Think about it." He picked up a nearby spanner and tapped it against his shin. It resounded with a high-pitched clink. He put the spanner back.

"Metal?"

"I had the bone replaced after it was all shattered up during a particularly nasty case back when I was a cop. Building collapse."

Understanding washed over me. "Why did you kill Robert?"

"I saw my chance and took it," he said. "I was trying to kill you; I was angry, just escaped from Professor Lowe's lab. But Robert, him and Jill, they'd slept together. Before. Before the accident. I decided it was better to keep you alive, so you could see what you've done. I just needed to keep you out of the way, so I framed you." He grinned. "It was the same with Sam's murder. We had fun with that one."

"You're insane," I said. It was all beginning to make sense. No wonder my life had felt out of place since the accident. I wasn't the right Jack Gemini. But this guy, this other me, he was a murderer. "You really are insane."

The other Jack shrugged. "You robbed me of the last three years and ruined my relationships. You took over where I left off. I was going to turn it all around, be a better cop, stop sleeping around and settle down. I was going to live!" He pointed at me. "But you... you pissed it all up the wall! What have you done since you got out of the vortex? Have you moved on? No. Have you improved yourself? No; you still drink, smoke and fuck your way through life. You use people. You took Jill from me. You took everything. And you're still the same piece of shit you were before the accident. You've flushed my life down the toilet! You haven't changed."

"And you have?"

"Yes, yes, I've changed. I'm a better man."

"Really? What have you done with your life since the accident? Obsess over the past? You're the one who needs to move on." I tried to adjust myself in the chair; I was losing the feeling in my hands and feet from the tight ropes and my wounded leg was making it worse. "Do you really have to destroy the world to put things right?"

"Destroy the world? Ha!"

"Did Lowe tell you what would happen? Did he tell you before you murdered him? This vortex, the one you're about to create, it'll become a black hole. It will consume Earth and everything around it."

"You have no idea what that bastard did to me, things that should've been done to you. You were the anomaly, but we were mixed up. And destroy the world? That's a risk I'm willing to take," said Subject B. "I don't have anything to lose."

"You could lose me," said Sam. "You told me you loved me."

"I... I do," said the other me. I wasn't convinced and I could tell by Sam's expression that he wasn't either. "I want us to have a life together," he implored. "I... I love you, Sam."

"Is it true?" said the bartender. "Is it true this could destroy everything?"

"That won't happen; I know what I'm doing."

"But there's a chance?"

"A small chance," said Subject B. "Trust me, Sam."

"Sam," I said, "he's going to kill us all."

"Shut up!"

"Tell me, Jack," I said, "just how will recreating the vortex fix things? There's two of us. So what? There has to be a place in this universe for both of us. It's big enough. We're not the same person anymore; three years is a long time, a long time for us to both change. And the more time that passes, the more different we become." My leg was losing blood fast; Sam had kicked it hard enough to make the liquid bandage ineffective. "You don't have to do this; we can both live."

"Everything will go back the way it should be," said Subject B. He stepped off the platform and headed to a control panel on another machine. "You'll see. You'll both see."

When did I become so crazy? I thought to myself. "And what happens after you switch on the machine?" I said. "How does that make everything go back the way it should be?"

The other man shrugged. "It just will." He turned away from me and started to push buttons on the equipment. Beeps and whirrs increased in their regularity. It was beginning. The end of everything.

I looked to Sam. He still held the gun in my direction, but he was looking at the other Jack Gemini.

"You look worried," I said to him. "Are you sure about this?"

"Yes." His attention was still on Subject B. "We're in love, which is more than you and I were."

"I loved you, Sam. In my own way, and I'm sorry I didn't show it soon enough." The blood was beginning to seep beneath my buttocks. "I know he told you he loves you. But, so did I."

"I love him, Jack. It doesn't matter how he feels about me."

"You loved me too; it still mattered when you shot me in the leg," I whispered. "And when you killed Jill. Have you told him about her? About how you shot her in cold blood? Do you really think he's going to forgive you for that?"

"I..."

"Sam," said Subject B. "Stop talking; he's just trying to get in your head." He grabbed a large switch with both hands and turned his head to look at the two of us. "Ready? Everything's going to be great again."

Subject B, the other Jack, the other me, pulled on the switch.

The two pillars sparked and ignited, and the machines roared to life.

"I love you, Sam," I said.

The vortex burst to life.

It was all over.

the final case of Jack Gemini

24. The Final Case of Jack Gemini

White light filled the lab. Blinding. The swirling vortex spun and undulated between the two pillars and cast its deadly illumination across the room. Deep shadows trailed across the floor, the darkest was Subject B's.

"I did it!" He laughed. "I goddamned did it!" He laughed again, harder this time. He was ecstatic. Crazed.

The smell of electrical burning and smoke filled my nostrils. This was it. This was the end of everything. Sparks ran up and down the pillars, arced across the machines, and skipped from panel to panel, jumped and danced. This wasn't like before.

Sam ducked in front of me. I felt his hands around my ankles, untying the ropes he'd bound me with.

"Fuck," he said. It was hard to hear him over the buzzing and whooshing of the dread portal in the middle of the wall. "I really did a number on your leg, didn't I?"

"There's no time," I said. "Quick." My legs were free. "My hands."

Sam darted behind me and my arms were freed. I snatched the gun from my former lover and aimed at the other me; it was time to end this.

I fired.

Subject B was ready; he ducked and rolled, and the bullet shot by his head and disappeared into the churning mass behind him. I only had moment to wonder at its fate. He had a gun of his own and he was the better aim. I felt his bullet pierce my shoulder. Goddammit. I shot back and he dived behind a desk. Another miss.

"You're too late," shouted the other man. "You can't stop it now."

I darted behind one of the machines and pulled Sam with me. Subject B was shooting again.

"You're hurt," said Sam. "Again."

"I know." I clutched my shoulder. My hand was barely containing the blood.

"Is there anything I can do?"

I shook my head. "Stay back." I leaned out and fired a few more shots at Subject B. Each was a miss.

"Sam!" My twin called out. "How could you do this to me? How could you betray me?" Bullets ricocheted to my left. "I trusted you! And you run back to him?"

The machines around us chugged; I could feel the static building in the atmosphere. There was little time left.

"If you loved me," Sam replied, "you'd stop this, Jack. You're going to end it all!"

"Jack," I chimed in. It was odd, calling my own name. "There has to be a way to work things out, a way for us both to move on."

"Don't do this," said the man to my right. "Please."

The other Jack didn't reply; he didn't shoot at me either. I only heard the resonating thrum of the environment around me. Electric ignited, drifted its tendrils through the air. The white light of the vortex burnt itself through every corner.

"Jack?" I said. "You need to let it go. Move on. You're gonna goddamned kill everyone!"

"I'll do whatever it takes." More gunshots bounced against my metal shield.

"Are you going to kill Sam?"

The gunfire was sufficient enough to indicate his answer. I glanced at Sam; tears were running down his face. He was heartbroken. Again.

"Sam…" I said. "I… I…"

"It's okay," he said. "It really is. He's a killer." He touched my face and smiled. "So am I."

"Sam, I've killed people too, you know. You don't have to…"

"I'm sorry, Jack, I really am. I'm sorry about everything." He kissed me, passionately and deeply. I'd forgotten how good he felt. "I'm sorry about Jill." He smiled again, his tears sparkling in the white light.

"What are you doing?" I asked. "You're not going to do anything stupid, are you?"

He stroked my cheek and shrugged.

Sam dived out from the cover and across to a table just across from me. He wasn't seen by the other me, I hoped, but, just in case, I fired a few rounds in Subject B's direction.

"Sam!" I hissed. "Sam! Don't do this!"

He waved his hand at me to dismiss me. He shuffled away from me and ducked under the stairwell. He was lucky the lab was so bright, so full of other distractions; his shadow was disguised amongst the monstrous and tumultuous light assaulting the room. There was no stopping him; I needed to take out Subject B before Sam could get any closer.

"Jack!" I shouted above the hum. "Stop this! The police are on their way!" I hoped. I really hoped they were. "You have to stop this now." I fired a few rounds around the corner. "We don't have to do this! We shouldn't be fighting!"

His maniacal laugh displaced the shrieks and cacophony from the machines, the roar from the vortex. He really had lost his mind, hadn't he?

He shot at me again.

I could see Sam anymore. He'd disappeared in the glare and I prayed to whatever gods were listening that he wasn't going to do what I thought he was going to do.

I had to stop Subject B now.

I leapt from my hiding place and fired... nothing. The gun was empty.

"Fuck..." I dropped behind the table where Sam had been and narrowly avoided another shower of bullets that came my way. I almost slipped in my own blood. "Damn, damn, damn!"

I peeked over the top.

"You're out of ammo," said the other me. He stood. "There's nothing you can do, you know." He walked forward, out from his cover. "I've won." His gun raised toward my peeping head. "This is the end."

Sam stood and spoke up. "Jack?" he said. He took a few steps toward his lover.

Subject B turned toward him. His expression changed from rage to concern.

"Jack, I have to tell you something," said Sam. "I want to know if you'll forgive me."

"Forgive you?" said the other man. "I... I love you Sam. I know you're confused but you're meant to be with me. Not him."

"I killed her, Jack."

"Who?" His face dropped. He knew. "Who did you kill?"

"I killed her. I killed Jill."

"Sam... no..." I could see his heart break from here, as mine had. "Sam..." There were tears in his eyes. He raised the gun toward the skinny man.

"You couldn't let her go, could you?" said Sam.

I heard the gun's hammer click back.

And then Sam screamed; he charged forward and tackled Subject B. The pair staggered backwards. He fought back, pushing and hitting the bartender to try and free himself from the embrace. It was no good. The gun clattered to the floor as the pair spun and danced in the surging light, screaming and grunting as they fought for control, their shadows mimicking their movement. Sam screamed again. Pushed. Barrelled against the other man's torso. Subject B was overpowered, and the two men fell into one of the pulsating pillars that straddled the spinning phenomenon.

The air crackled and burned. The smell of burning flesh assailed the room. The white light pulsed faster and faster and the surrounding equipment churned and ground harder than ever before.

And then, silence, darkness.

It was over.

I rose from behind the table and looked at the charred remains of my former lover and my other self. Something glinted in amongst the blackened bodies. My wedding ring. His. I couldn't take it. Not now.

I walked forward and dropped to my knees.

Tears fell down my cheeks. And I'd lost a lot of blood.

I laid down on my back. I could feel the blood still pouring from my shoulder and thigh.

Suede and Johnson should be here soon.

I hoped.

Subject B, the person whose life I'd inextricable stolen, was left only a burnt-out husk. His plans, the destructive vortex, gone. I'd taken his life. Sam had taken it too. A life that wasn't mine; I decided there and then that I needed to make the most of it. Make it mine.

For Sam.

And Jill.

Jack Gemini was dead.

But I still lived.

For now.

I shut my eyes and dreamed that, somewhere, somehow, maybe in the other world, my parallel world, Jill and Sam were both happy.

I drifted away.

Case Closed.

the final case of Jack Gemini

the final case of Jack Gemini

the final case of Jack Gemini

10b. Accident

8 years ago.

Earth.

Augustus Smith. The Emerald Killer. It wasn't my case, but I'd become involved. I was the nearest cop to the sighting. And I was alone. No partner. My old partner, Robert, had transferred to Space Station Delta. I didn't blame him, not after the last case we did together; it was a nasty one. He'd come out of it fine but the bones in my leg had been decimated and a metal replacement was the only option. It'd had shaken him up. Desk work was in his future. My new partner, on the other hand, I'd forgotten his name, I'd told him I needed to speak to an informant alone and like a good little newbie he'd complied. It was lie. I'd lied to my new partner. There'd been a good reason. Well, not a particularly good reason, but a reason. There were some things a cop had to do without the watchful eyes of a partner; it was something not wholly legal. And now I'd been dragged into something big. Goddammit. I didn't know why I'd responded to the call; I could've just carried on with my side business and pretended I didn't hear it.

The problem was that I'd checked in with HQ about thirty minutes previous; they knew I was in the industrial district and if I hadn't responded it would have garnered nothing but suspicion. I didn't need the hassle. There were already rumours in the station that I was under investigation and I didn't want to add more fuel to the fire they were building.

I headed out with some haste. Smith had been seen in the area, clearly seen by the surveillance cameras and not by some fuzzy witness who may or may not have seen someone with the resemblance to the killer. It was a reckless move by Smith; from what I understood about the case, he was careful. Usually. Some of the more proficient and respectable detectives had been on the case for almost a year and had gotten no closer to catching the notorious killer. I'd tried to stay out of it, but I guess it was now my turn to get involved. The Emerald Killer had been the talk of the town, the talk of the station and the media for too long thanks to his unusual penchant for leaving a green circle on the foreheads of his victims. Every person, man, woman or other, had one thing in common: green eyes. It was Smith's creepy little fetish. Sicko.

I headed for the outskirts of the district; he'd been sighted near some large facility that mounted the boundary between the industrial sector and commercial. I didn't know much about it, only that HQ was very concerned that Smith had been seen near it.

I was going to be the good cop today.

I shouldn't even be chasing a known killer like Smith without back up, but here I was. Dammit, why did I choose now to do the right thing? Well, not the right thing, just the right thing to keep the station's eyes from my dodgy dealing; I could imagine the look on all their faces if I actually managed to catch Augustus Smith.

Me.

Doing my job.

Ha.

Ha. Ha.

I checked in with dispatch; back up was still an hour away. It was definitely all up to me to catch him. If I didn't, I didn't. No skin off my nose. I just had to try. And not get killed. My death was unlikely; I didn't have green eyes, but I could still end up as collateral damage.

The streets of the industrial district were quiet. They always were this time of night. Or morning. All I knew was that it was late and there was no-one about but hookers and druggies. And myself. And, of course, the killer.

I kept my eyes open, trying not to give the whores any attention, and scanned the streets for Smith. This was the street he'd been seen on and there didn't seem to be any sign of him now.

I might be too late.

It might be worth speaking to Candice. She was usually working around here and she owed me a favour or two.

I approached one of the rent boys to my left; he probably thought I was looking for some trade, but I never paid for my affairs. At least, not with money.

"Hey," I said.

"You looking for something, mister?" He fluttered his scabbed eyes at me. He did not look too healthy. There were blisters around his mouth too.

"Yeah, I'm looking for Candice. Is she about tonight?"

"Who's asking?"

"Tell her it's an old friend who needs a favour."

"Candice has a lot of friends," said the sex worker. "You smell like a cop." His breath was vile. "You could be anyone."

"Trust me," I said, "she knows me." I slipped him a couple of notes. Cash was on its way out, but it was always worth carrying a few credits worth. Cash was untraceable.

He nodded, subtly, but he understood. "I still need a name."

"Tell her it's Jack."

The rent boy moved a little back from me to put a message through on his SmartBoy. Candice wasn't the type to keep me waiting. Still, I was attracting some suspicious looks from the other whores and I tried to keep my eyes elsewhere; I didn't want to attract any of their pimps, at least, the pimps other than Candice. She had a pretty good relationship with the other 'self-employed' around this area and I certainly didn't want to get on the bad side of any of them. I was taking a chance by asking for Candice in the open like this; she usually liked to keep things private because she had a reputation to uphold. It didn't look good if she was seen cavorting with cops. Even ones like me. But she did owe me a lot of favours.

"She didn't sound happy," said the boy as he approached. "She didn't sound at all happy."

"I thought as much," I said.

He raised his eyebrows expectantly.

"Oh, right." I slipped him a few more notes.

He spoke in a whisper. "Meet her around the corner in the alley; she's waiting for you."

"This isn't going to be some sort of trap, is it?" I joked. "Where I turn the corner and get a beating?"

"That service costs more," he said with a wink. He smiled; it was awkward, and I got the feeling he was trying to be seductive. "If you're here again, come and look me up."

I reluctantly nodded and moved away. I headed for the alley with the full knowledge that the rent boy was watching my ass.

I turned the corner. There was no crowd of thugs waiting for me, just a fancy black car.

I recognised it immediately as one of Candice's collection; she had a lot of vehicles.

A bejewelled arm waved from a rear window and beckoned me closer. All the glass of the car was tinted, almost black, but I knew who waited within.

"Good evening, my queen," I said; I gave her an exaggerated bow. "And, how are you this lovely evening?"

"Cut the bullshit, Jack." She wore her usual thick wallpaper paste make-up; it didn't act as much of a disguise because she was never seen without it. "I think I know why you're here."

"Oh, really?"

She nodded. The plenitude of earrings and fascinators jangled loudly. "You here because of Augustus Smith."

"You've heard." It didn't surprise me; the painted whoremonger always knew what was going on where her girls and boys worked, even when she shouldn't. Candice always knew. I didn't know what or who her source was, but at a guess it was one of her high-profile johns.

"It seems once again our interests line up."

"Then you can owe me a favour another time," I said. "If this is for your benefit too."

"Oh, don't get me wrong, Jack," said Candice, "you get nothing in this life for free."

"Don't I know it."

The woman leant forward amidst a cacophony of rattling trinkets. "My little ones are in danger as long as he's around here; Marcus and Genevieve, two of my best, have green eyes, and I've had to take them off the streets for tonight. This Emerald Killer is costing me money."

"You and me, both," I replied. "I had to walk away from a very important deal for this shit."

"I expect you want to know where he is?"

"Why else would I come to you?"

"I thought it was for my sexy smile," she grinned through ruby lips. Her smile dropped. "I'm sure you can find a way for Smith to have an unfortunate accident."

"I'll let the law handle him," I said. "I'm not a killer."

"Morally bankrupt. Just push your morals a little more; you can do it. He's too dangerous and he'll just get caught up in the system; the law won't stop him, you know it won't."

"Tell me where he is."

She sighed. "He's hiding out in the Tribeca Systems building."

"The what?"

"Hand me your SmartBoy." She snatched it from my hand as soon as it left my pocket; she tapped in some directions and handed it back. "You really don't come this way often enough, as often as I'd like."

"I'll make more of an effort next time. It's hard. I've got to think about Jill."

Candice laughed. "Everyone knows you don't give a fuck about her; you've had more side pieces than a gun enthusiast."

"I'm trying."

"Don't say I didn't try to tell you otherwise," said the woman. She moved back into the darkened car and her arm ornaments faded from view; I could still hear them rattle. Like wind chimes.

I made my goodbyes and headed in the direction she'd laid out for me. She called out to me as the car's engine started up.

"Don't get yourself killed, Jack," she shouted.

Her vehicle disappeared and I was left alone with all the whores on the main street. I picked up my pace; Smith wouldn't stay there long. He was at the large facility he'd been seen near, the one straddling this sector and the next. Tribeca Systems. I didn't know too much about the company except that they were in the energy business. Power generation was very lucrative right now, especially with the looming energy crisis. It didn't help that most of the planet's population had abandoned this stinking place and emigrated to one of the space stations in orbit. I didn't blame them. Earth was turning into a garbage dump.

I reached the imposing building in very little time and quickly checked in with headquarters. Back-up was still thirty minutes away, a bullshit estimate; there was some sort of big accident on one of the highways keeping them busy. Augustus Smith, the Emerald Killer, did not seem to be their priority right now. It'd become mine.

Just my goddamned luck.

My next problem was finding a way in. The main entrance was fortified with big electric gates. A definite no-no. I started moving around to the right of the building looking for any indication there was a way in, or, indeed, any indication of where Smith had entered.

Inextricably, I found what I was looking for. It was almost too easy, almost as if the path had been laid out for me. I didn't like it. There was a ladder leaning against the wall, and at the top, a broken window.

Did Augustus Smith know someone was after him? Was this all a trap?

My instincts, worn away by years of incompetence, were telling me not to climb the ladder; they were telling me not to go after Smith. To wait for back up.

But how good would it look if I caught the notorious killer all on my lonesome?

This was a bad idea.

I didn't know what had come over me. I was never one to do things for the glory or adoration; I only did things for myself, to save my own hide. I was only doing this to keep the prying eyes of the precinct away from my... other dealings.

I stepped onto the ladder and climbed. It wasn't a high window, but it was tall enough to need assistance to reach it. I made sure my gun was loose in its holster; I wasn't taking any chances. I needed to be ready. Ready for whatever was waiting for me inside. The main lights were off and only the green safety lighting was providing any sort of illumination within. Smith had picked a good place to hide out. A quiet building in the middle of nowhere. It was surprising that there was no security about. Especially for a facility run by a big company. Cost-cutting always had its downsides.

Then again, it was probably all automated. They might have some of those fancy robot security guards with the broken A.I. They were popular amongst a lot of businesses, usually because they were so cheap. But they never worked as intended. More often than I'd like I'd be called out to a burglary only to discover the 'security' guard had arrested a mop. Or in one instance, half a dead cat.

And if Smith was inside, as Candice had told me, it was unlikely that the automated guard had gone anywhere near him.

I clambered through the window and emerged into a bathroom. My foot, conveniently, took a wash in the toilet bowl, and I was left with a sodden sock and trouser leg. That was great. At least the toilet was clean. I hoped. It was hard to tell in this light. There was certainly nothing solid floating around in the bowl, but the green lighting told me nothing of the water colour. I tried not to think about it as I moved from the stall to the door and into the hallway. I was probably going to end up leaving tracks along this flooring, the tracks of a one-legged man with a penchant for toilet water. Thankfully, I wasn't the one being tracked; I was the tracker. It seemed, that if Smith had come into the building the same way as me, he hadn't made the same mistake. There were no wet footprints leading away from the bathroom. I'd needed to decide which way to go.

I took a guess and headed left. I drew my gun in anticipation of a confrontation.

I could hear the distant grind and whir of machinery as I moved along the corridor. Something big and loud had been left running throughout the night and it was a mystery what it was; I didn't have a clue what Tribeca was doing in this facility. It was a large building and Smith could be anywhere. Maybe, if I could find the security control room, which managed the security cameras and guards, if the building had them, then I might be able to track down where the Emerald Killer was hiding. I didn't have a schematic or map of this place. It was going to be easy to get lost and there was a strong chance I'd probably end up finding Smith before I even got close to finding the control room.

I tested one or two doors as I made my way along the corridor. Locked. Smith could be in any one of the rooms, but there was no way of forcing the locks quietly, and if I shot at them, I would alert him to my presence. All I could do is move forward. And be ready in case he jumped out from behind me.

The mechanical humming grew louder and as I reached the end of the corridor I was greeted by a set of large double doors. A metal gangway lay beyond, and, in the verdant light, I could see a large, warehouse-sized room filled with complicated and confusing machinery, and whatever it was, there was another hue to the illumination; an undulating white light emanated deeper inside.

If Smith was in there, it was going to be a nightmare finding him. The facility was large enough already, but this room was going to have a lot of nooks and crannies tucked between and behind the strange apparatus.

I opened one of them double doors slowly and slightly and slipped carefully through. I paused, scanned the room and looked for any sign of my quarry. Nothing. At least, nothing obvious. There was at least some evidence he'd been here; below the gangway the broken body of a robot security guard lay mangled with its servos and gears spilt across the floor. Smith could be close. I needed to be careful.

I took a few steps onto the gangway; there was nowhere else to go. Except backwards, and I wasn't going to do that. The metal grating creaked beneath my feet. The noise made me feel uneasy. An omen? Almost as if the squeaks and groans were warning me that the walkway was going to shift and collapse beneath me; I really didn't want to end up like the security guard.

I moved forward, gun in hand, expecting Smith to jump me. I kept looking, scanning, surveying the room below for the notorious killer, but there was no sign of him anywhere. Aside from evidence of his destruction, the robot. The equipment ground and whirred beneath my feet and the white glow I'd seen before I'd entered the chamber was revealed.

A large spinning vortex of white light was pinned between two pillars. It didn't quite look right. Like it wasn't there and was there at the same time. The light swirled and spiralled and it almost seemed as if it occupied more than the usual three dimensions. It was impossible. Mesmerising. It was difficult to keep my eyes off it.

I shook my head to clear its hypnotism from my vision. I needed to focus.

I tried to work out what I was seeing. The strange glowing whirlpool of light was being brewed by the machines around it, ignited from the tall pillars. The vortex was prominent, the whole purpose of this facility. Sparks trickled and caressed the surrounding contraptions, feeding the weird phenomenon. Or being fed by it.

I turned away from the entrancing light and continued along the gangway. I was beginning to feel uneasy. My instincts were screaming at me to run and I didn't know whether it was the effects of the odd vortex, radiation or whatever, or if the Emerald Killer was close.

There was another door ahead, and, to its left, a metal staircase leading down to the chamber floor.

I had a choice. Search this room. Or move on.

I ignored my gut and took the stairs. They were just as arthritic as the gangway, and I managed to get to the bottom without structural collapse and broken bones.

The machines were deafening, and the vibrations echoed through the soles of my feet; my ears hummed in synch with their sinister machinations. The battered robot was just ahead. I approached its metal corpse, making sure to scan the room for Smith as I neared. If he was here, he was doing a good job at remaining unseen.

The spinning illumination caught my attention again and I found myself turning toward it. I moved closer, bewitched by the spinning lights. A slope led down to the trench in which it filled, and I found myself getting near. This close, it seemed even more unreal, taking up more space than just this room. There seemed to be something drawing me closer. Pulling me. Inevitability? I wasn't sure. I didn't want to get any closer, but I couldn't keep my eyes from the spinning lights of the singularity before me.

I slipped and fell forward.

White filled my vision.

the final case of Jack Gemini

FREE SAMPLE

He had a thing for Virgins and other stories

the final case of Jack Gemini

EARL GREY WITH GINGERBREAD BISCUITS

"Really Ethel, I don't know how you can live in a place like this." Her guest, one of her oldest and dearest friends, shook out her coat and hung it up on the little coat rack by the door. "That's another pair of expensive shoes ruined."

"I've told you before and I'm telling you again," she said, ushering her friend to the sofa. They seemed to go through the same ritual every fortnight when she came in from the city. "Shoes like that aren't fit to walk through the woods in; you should buy a decent pair of boots." She clicked her heels. "Like these."

"Me? Seen in those hideous things? I think not."

"It's that or keep ruining your fancy shoes. Just 'cos it looks pretty don't mean it's practical."

"One must keep up appearances dear. Polite society would shun me. Shun me, Ethel."

"Mavis," she hobbled over to the door leading into the kitchen, "it's not like you can't afford to keep buying new shoes. I'll go get the tea; the kettle just whistled before you knocked."

"Earl Grey today?" She heard Mavis shout from the lounge. "I really fancy a bit of Earl Grey."

"Yes dear." She popped a couple of tea bags into the pot and poured on the hot water. She picked out her fanciest tea cosy and dressed the pot before placing it on the tray containing her most delicate china. "How are the daughters?" She always used her best crockery when Mavis visited.

"Don't ask."

"That bad dear?" She made sure the biscuits were arranged neatly before heading back to the lounge. She placed the tray on the table and sat on the edge of her armchair. "I thought your eldest were doing really well?" She lifted the teapot.

"Oh, the two eldest girls are wonderful. They've been excited about the big fancy do on Saturday." Mavis daintily picked up a slice of lemon and dropped it in her cup. "No sugar, love; I'm trying to cut down."

"Has that meddling old doctor been up in your drawers again?" She poured some tea into her own cup and dropped in a sugar cube. The spoon clinked against the china as she stirred.

"No, no nothing like that. Need to start looking after myself; getting old Ethel."

"Aren't we all," she said, dropping in a second sugar cube. "And what about your youngest?"

She sighed. "Trying my patience." Her friend took a sip from her cup. "She's just so lazy. Never does her chores properly; I really don't know what I'm going to do with her. And you know the worst part? She keeps letting mice into the house! Tells me she feels sorry for them and they need a home too. She feeds them. Bloody vermin."

"Language, Mavis." Ethel sat back in the chair and took in the aromatic scent of her tea. "It sounds like you need to give that girl a little chastising. Teach her a lesson. She's in your house; she's got to show some respect." She waved her hand over the plate of biscuits. "Help yourself to some biscuits."

"Well, she's already banned from leaving the house. And I've told her she is not to go to the do with her sisters." Mavis reached for the tray and paused. "Really, dear? Gingerbread men? After I told you what happened to that baker the last time I was here?"

She giggled. "Oh come on Mavis, you've got to let me have a little bit of fun now and again."

"It's morbid is what it is, Ethel." The old woman picked up one of the little men and took a bite. "Mmm. Fair play, you've outdone yourself again; you'll have to give me the recipe."

"See?" She took a little tipple of her own tea. "We're not too old to keep enjoying ourselves."

"You know Hyacinth's girl? She's still living in that cottage." Mavis put the one-legged man on the saucer with her cup. "With those men. Helping them clean up the place apparently."

"Well I never! It's not right. A young girl shacked up with a bunch of old men! If you ask me, she's doing more than polishing their ornaments. Disgusting!"

"Ethel!"

269

"Well, what else is she doing there? I heard they all sleep in the same room."

"I'm sure it's all innocent. They are old men after all; they probably can't look after themselves."

"I know what's she looking after. We all know what men are like."

"Ethel!"

"It's her poor mother I feel sorry for; it can't be easy with the father gone."

"I know, dear. I've struggled since losing Henry."

"I'm sorry, Mavis." She patted her friend's knee. "I didn't mean to bring it up like that."

"Quite alright." The old woman took another nibble of the gingerbread. The other leg. "You know Hyacinth tried to go to talk to her? Bring her home."

"Really?"

"Oh yes. But you know what that little upstart said to her? Told her to go take a long walk off a short cliff!"

"Girls these days don't know any respect."

"It's terrible. Hyacinth is so worried about her; she's been sneaking apples down to her from the orchard."

"And the girl was rude to her?"

Mavis nodded and pursed her lips. "It's all going to end in misery, mark my words."

"Oh my." Ethel took another sip of tea. The cup was almost empty. "Did you hear about what happened to poor old Gertrude?"

"Is she back in hospital again? She's always so sickly; stuck in that bed in the middle of nowhere with no family close. All alone in that forest. Like you. And, Ethel, her granddaughter is the only one who goes to visit her. Poor thing. It's a wonder no wolves have gobbled her up."

"Brace yourself, dear. Something horrible happened." She leaned forward and filled up her cup from the pot. "Allegedly, it's all that grandchild's fault. She was murdered, Mavis."

"No?!"

"Oh yes dear. Murder."

"And the granddaughter did it?"

"Well, apparently she was getting it on with one of the woodcutters. He said he did it for her. To save her. Sliced Gertrude open with his axe." She drew a line across her belly with her finger. "Cut her wide open and spilled her insides everywhere."

"Ethel, please don't be so tasteless. You're going to put me off my tea."

"The things people do for love. It's a sick world, Mavis."

"That poor woman. She didn't have it easy." She brought her cup up to her lips. "Well, I suppose that's why the girl was the only one going to visit her, if you know what I mean." She shook herself. "It's just all so gruesome. What a horrible thing to bring up."

"Just keeping you up to date, dear." Ethel leaned forward and picked up one of the gingerbread men. "Anyway, it's no worse than what you told me about that young man last time." She bit off the head.

271

"Breaking into that man's house, robbing him blind. And then when he got caught…"

"That's a little bit different, Ethel."

"I don't see how. The mess after falling from that height!"

"That young boy was desperate. Now, I'm not saying it's any excuse for what he did, but he got conned out of some money, and his poor mother and him were starving. They had nothing. It's just unfortunate he turned to crime."

"Still…"

"Murder is a very different thing to theft, my dear."

"True. True." She took another bite of the biscuit. "But you can't excuse what he did, Mavis." She washed it down with a little more tea.

"No."

Ethel topped up her friend's cup. "Any news on George's daughter?"

"Not much." She snuck a sugar cube into her cup.

"Sugar, Mavis?"

She tapped her finger on her lip with a smirk. "She's still living with that beast of a man. Such a pretty girl too."

"I've heard the rumours. Heard he's rich."

"Very. Lives in a big mansion, but he's not a pleasant man from what I hear. Bit of a temper. Not very well-endowed in the looks department."

the final case of Jack Gemini

"I can see why people think she's only there for the money."

"Well, Ethel, she told her father that it's true love. She said it's more important than looks."

"Mmhmm." She dipped one of the gingerbread man's legs into her tea and crunched it between her teeth. "But that's all very well, dear, but there has to be a limit."

"George told me she was engaged to some fella in the village before. Big handsome fella."

"Money over looks eh? I suppose she's thinking of the future. Looks fade."

"You haven't seen him, Ethel."

"That bad?"

"Oh yes." Her friend sipped at the cup. "Beast of a man."

"Oh dear oh dear." She shook her head. "Girls these days, Mavis."

"The men are just as bad. It wasn't like this when we were gals."

"No dear."

"Anyway, Ethel." She finished off the tea in her cup and placed the crockery onto the table. "I must be going." She stood. "Got to go sort out the girl's dresses and get their shoes from the shoemaker. And get myself some new shoes."

Ethel stood, brushing the crumbs from her apron. "Where is this fancy do then?"

"At the castle." She strode over to the door and picked up her coat from the hook. "The prince is hosting."

"I can see why shoes are important."

"Why?" She slipped her arms in the sleeves.

"Well, I'm sure you heard about the prince."

"I'm sure whatever you've heard, Ethel, it's just rumour."

"He's got a bit of a... you know... about feet."

"Really Ethel, you can't believe everything you hear."

"I'll have you know, Mavis, that I heard this from a very good source. He likes his ladies' shoes, that prince. Especially after they've been worn."

Her friend's face scrunched up in disgust as she pulled her coat over her shoulders and adjusted it.

"You never know," said Ethel, "might get you in with the royal family if one of your girls wears the right shoes."

"I shall bear that in mind." She reached for the door and opened it.

"Don't be a stranger, Mavis." The two old friends exchanged air kisses. "I do look forward to your visits."

"As do I, dear. As do I." Mavis stepped out the door and looked around. "You know, Ethel, I don't know how you keep this house so nice. It must be difficult with all the animals around."

"It's not the animals you've got to worry about; it's the kids."

"No respect."

"I know, I know. Anyway, take care and enjoy your fancy do. I've got to get the oven preheated for later. Having the grandkids for dinner."

"Take care dear."

She waved to her friend and closed the gingerbread door.

The End.

the final case of Jack Gemini

ABOUT THE AUTHOR

T. A. Jenkins is an author famous for... well... nothing. But he does write things. Sometimes. When not tending to the fertile fields of procrastination, T. A. Jenkins can be found either on Twitter (@norab84) or alternatively, somewhere in South Wales pretending to get some writing done.

the final case of Jack Gemini